THE CLASS OF MISS MACMICHAEL

An explosive, irreverent and brilliantly-characterized novel, originally published as **EFF OFF.**

Sandy Hutson

The Class of Miss MacMichael

Originally published as EFF OFF

CORGI BOOKS
A DIVISION OF TRANSWORLD PUBLISHERS LTD

THE CLASS OF MISS MACMICHAEL

A CORGI BOOK 0 552 10819 7

Originally published in Great Britain as 'Eff Off'
by Arlington Books (Publishers) Ltd.

PRINTING HISTORY

Arlington Books edition published 1969
Corgi edition published 1978

This book is set in 11–11½pt Intertype Baskerville

Corgi Books are published by
Transworld Publishers Ltd.,
Century House, 61–63 Uxbridge Road,
Ealing, London W5 5SA
Made and printed in Great Britain by
Cox & Wyman Ltd., London, Reading and Fakenham

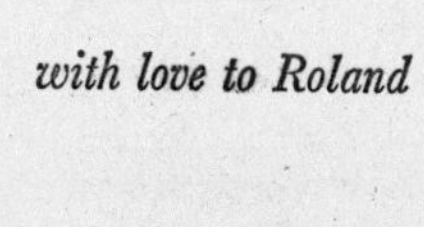

with love to Roland

CHAPTER ONE

THE tannoy belched. Seamus' voice split the tangled maze of tension in my classroom.

'Gaylord, man, get down out of that tree, now. I'm going to be away for the next half-hour and I want everyone working while I'm gone. Gaylord, God dammit, get out of that tree or I'll belt the crap out of you. Hear me?'

It was almost noon and, apparently, he wanted Gaylord out of the tree so that he could go to the pub for a drink.

I struggled to cut Boysie's black hair, my elbows ripping on the metallic tension that filled the classroom. I used the school's sole pair of scissors which, blunt, blades caked with glue, one tip broken, and gilded with rust, were a symbolic banner of this educational institution. Some haircut.

'I'll ask you once more, Stewart, will you fucking well clean up that cat?' Boysie's voice wound around my blotting-paper brain and sprawled on the litterbin, as his barometer eyes gradually filmed and dropped towards opaque.

Stewart slouched, watching us, feet on my desk, a mangled matchstick dangling from his sullen mouth. He spat a sticky wad of morose silence at his classmate. I beat ineffectually at the swollen clot of strain.

'Stewart, you painted the cat with aluminium paint and she'll die, if she licks it off. She's only a baby kitten. Go clean it off now.'

No one listened, and my words filed neatly into the litterbin to die slowly of emotional poisoning. The gummy scissors, furred with black hair, chewed valiantly at the tangled mass. Sunlight spewed through the dirty window, pushing around the knotted silence of the room. No one moved. No one spoke. The air congealed.

The classroom door banged open and my eyes focused around the tidal wave of tension.

'Bernie, get out. We're busy at the moment.'

'Bugger off, you fucking pro.'

She lounged against the jamb, avidly digesting the scene with her gangrenous gut. Blue eyes, smudged with jet-black liner, glinted behind a tangled stack of bleached hair that drooled down over her tight sweater. Shiny platinum lips parted, releasing her customary shriek. I staggered, pierced through the throat.

'Ooh, oh, he's having his itsy bitsy curls cut ism?'

A rising crescendo of spasmodic cackles accompanied the slow rotation of her mammoth bosom. Two myopic teak chips died behind the thick spectacles as Boysie sprang from his chair and sent the front desk skidding across the room. Splintering a chair on the ageing sink, Boysie shot towards the doorway, stumbling over the silver cat, who cowered licking at the aluminium. Bernie's wanton face sparkled in childish excitement at this coveted, but unexpected, attention and she fled down the corridor, shrieking. Scissors and I fused in benumbed, granite jelly.

The front door banged, shattering a pane of glass. Bernie's screech settled to a prolonged wail and I saw her streak past my window towards the woods, pursued by Boysie as he tried desperately to overtake her, one broken chair leg upraised.

Sun drops spattered the air and split dry leaves into fragments. Summer growth on the trees bordering the school shrivelled in the warmth and spiralled down towards the untended growth of brambles and grass. Branches of the trees in the school wood intertwined above the brook and cradled the October breeze.

Stewart picked his teeth lethargically. I could hear Marrie's shout from the girls' loo:

'Get out of here, you dirty fucking moo.'

Someone thudded against the corridor wall.

I rolled out an untasted emotion and sat down.

'Aint'cha going out after 'em?' Stewart threw his matchstick at the blackboard.

'No, why should I?'

'Cause you're the teacher, aint'cha?'

A teacher who doesn't teach in limbo disguised as a school. A supporting actor whose immediate role in the corrosive drama is to run ineffectually through the wood after two temporarily demented students in a pointless, but dramatic, gesture of constant vigilance and efficiency. I didn't move.

Sun and silence settled comfortably on the clutter that filled my cramped classroom. Desks were squeezed together a few inches from the blackboard in order to provide space for eight enormous workbenches in the back of the room. A carpenter's delight, the benches were constructed of heavy oak and each boasted a vice, slots for tools, and spacious storage shelves. None of the staff were qualified to teach woodwork and the benches had mouldered, unused, in this room for years. Two potters' wheels, never used, rusted against locked and barred french doors. A tall, battered tool chest, infant school games, egg-boxes, dustbins, chests of drawers, and an assortment of unidentifiable objects rotted in forgotten heaps, piling to the ceiling, blocking windows and obstructing the doors. There were no lockers, no bookcases and no cupboards, although there was a sink for which I had no use. It was a refuse dump.

Boysie's shadow flitted past the window again and the front door crashed, splintering a second pane of glass. Teak eyes and a black mane threw themselves across the room at Stewart who still slumped at my desk.

'That cat, you fucker. Miss told you to clean up the cat.'

Stewart was jerked across the desk and flung, headlong, against the wall. Enraged and out of control, Boysie crushed the boy into the crumbling plaster, smashing his head repeatedly against the wall. Stewart crumpled to the floor and Boysie jerked him up again, twisting the swollen throat. A kick sent Stewart hurtling through the doorway, rolling down the corridor, bouncing from one side of the hallway to the other. A gush of fear frizzed the nerves in my spinal cord, splashing my mind with tepid ammonia and jerking my legs into an involuntary run after the battered boy. Boysie passed me and dragged Stewart into the boys' lavatory.

'Get out of the way! Let me in! Move!'

They could feel trouble, smell fear, taste dislike. They accepted one another unquestioningly, fused together by the demoralizing knowledge that they were the Rejects of Society. The fabric of their lives was finely woven of trouble and violence, and their unvarying reaction to any disturbance at school was predictable. Clustering about the brawl they stood silently, watching with newspaper eyes. Not one interfered with the combatants and none spoke of the incident later. Three brass monkeys, chattering noiselessly skittered through the rows of inanimate spectators, transforming them into a deaf, speechless carving.

I clawed my way through the crowd and fell inside the doorway. Stewart's head was in the toilet. Boysie pulled the chain.

'Now you bloody well clean that cat!'

I hooked a finger through Boysie's belt and pulled him backwards as he aimed one final, aggressive kick at Stewart. The heavy motorcycle boot connected with an aged pipe in the urinal which broke as it ripped from the wall. A fetid mixture of urine, cigarette butts and slimy water spewed about the room, reviving Stewart who crawled through the doorway. Boysie hunched his shoulders and asked,

'How about the haircut?'

'Sure. Oh, sure.'

We dripped from the loo, my right eyeball floating in a rancid pool of urine. The only sound was the crackle of translucent statues, still standing mute and observant, outside the lavatory door. Mabel, the Deputy Head, magnetized by the thrill of trouble, had joined the students, and she pulled thick lips back over her giant teeth indicating sympathy for everyone. You bitch.

Boysie strutted back to the classroom, slung a towel over his sepia shoulders and sat down. I trailed behind him, wringing urine from my skirt and picking tobacco shreds from my forehead. Prying open the scissors, I began to lacerate his hair.

Damn the scissors, damn the school. I give haircuts to most of the students here and I want some nice sharp barbers' shears and a new pair of clippers. I'm stamping around after the Holy Grail, too. I burped up an evil chuckle and Boysie twisted around in the chair.

'So what's up with you?'

'Sit still or I'll cut your ear.'

'You already done that.'

'Sorry.'

There won't be any new shears, not even for the kids and certainly not for me. The only thing we get for free here is a perpetual, noxious drama written, directed and produced by the star, our Headmaster.

Mowing through the black spikes I sighed. Some school. A state special school for maladjusted children. It sure was special. I had to buy all the pencils, paper and materials for my class. And books. There are no textbooks in the school. A roaming library on wheels appears irregularly during the year and it does have a wider selection of modern mystery stories for the adolescent girl, and adventure tales for every age. They aren't very hip in the textbook line, though. Maybe I should take advantage of what they do offer and teach my students about yeti tracking. They would be fascinated by that bit of practical knowledge. Oh God. The children are misfits, rotten scum, so hide them with us. They don't deserve good teachers or decent equipment or even a usable school building because they have never had those things and won't appreciate them. Save such luxuries for the normal children from innocuous homes, the quiet, respectful students who will grow up to be hardworking bricklayers, supporting three children and washing the economy car on Sundays. Bury the violent, the uncontrollable, the disturbed under our polythene stage. Give them nothing. Contain but don't teach. When they have reached the magic age of sixteen years it will be someone else's problem. Life's Rejects, serving a term as animated props in the paper theatre at St. Steven's School. But don't cut them because they bleed just like everyone else.

And the staff, the plastic puppets jerking on the ends of Seamus' steel string, basking in praise and esteem bestowed by a grateful society for bravely dealing with these wretched creatures by conspiring to conceal them from a public who doesn't want to know. Most of us are as unbalanced as the students, but it's difficult to determine whether this type of institution attracts the adult misfit or whether the school erodes an integrated personality, leaving a residue of naked neuroses.

Snip, snip, gouge. He was almost bald, and there were peculiar patches in the clipped hair, but it resembled a crew cut. And it was free.

'You're done, Boysie.'

'Yeah. Ta. I didn't even want to hit him, Miss. I just went spare. I was thinking about New Zealand again and it got on me wick.'

His family was emigrating at Christmas.

'I know, Boysie, and I'd like to help, but there's nothing that I or anyone else can do about it. You can come back in two years anyway.'

'Oh sure. Christ, I'll be old then. I'll be eighteen and

none of me mates will be up the Common. Christ!'

He bent over and beat the floor with his towel.

'Go take a shower. You've got that stuff all over you. And get a broom in here and sweep up the room. See what you can do about repairing the chair before Sir finds out that it's broken.'

'Lost the leg, didn't I?'

'Well, go find it!'

He loped out.

A spidery shadow squashed the sun drops on my window and crawled on towards the shattered front door, signalling Seamus' return from the pub. I gathered in my mutilated nerves and anaesthetized emotions, stuffed two holes in my shoe with newspaper and prepared to get into his office before anyone else. It was a standard regulation, dictated by the skirmish for survival and enforced by chiffon instability in this catatonic theatre-land.

I pushed my way down the hall, past Marrie screaming at Abel.

'You fucking moo! I saw you and Brooks having it off last Saturday at the Black Swan.'

She and Patty giggled, danced furiously just in front of their prey and darted into the girls' loo as he lunged forward. Convulsive laughter rolled around the lavatory and overflowed into the corridor where it bounced and reverberated on rusting pipes and cracked plaster.

'Slag.'

Two hands appeared around the doorway, flinging obscene signs in Abel's direction. He picked up a chair and heaved it towards the waving fingers. It bounced off the wall and ground, leg first, into my ribs. I crumpled, gagging as I tried desperately to suck air into my dissolving lungs. Crumbling corridor walls slanted and wavered forward, splashing in molten concrete chunks. Marrie's scream churned into a rising tunnel of indistinguishable, prolonged noise that exploded in one battered ear drum.

'Miss, your arm's in the fishtank.'

'Oh. Well help me, you fool.'

A tiny boy peeled me away from the fishtank as Abel galloped down the hallway and enveloped me in a massive squeeze that pushed the air from collapsing nerve ends and blistered raw ribs. Bands of coloured noise wrapped themselves around my brain as Abel and I began to spiral down the corridor. I struggled feebly to extricate myself from his crushing embrace.

'I'm sorry, Miss. I didn't see you. Really I didn't. It was for that fucking slag.'

'Abel, you're hurting me. It wouldn't happen if you didn't throw chairs. Abel I can't breathe. Get off!'

'All right, you old cow. Be like that.'

I staggered on to Seamus' office, hearing the happy sounds of a normal school day behind me.

'Moo! Moo!'

'Slag.'

'Piss off.'

I opened Seamus' door. I wasn't first. The staff had gathered and affixed appropriately sage expressions to plastic faces, implying that they extended sympathy to the winner. Whoever it might be.

Mabel brayed. She pursued the word 'inefficiency' around the room, trying to bite it to death and gave up when it jumped into my ear. Fat lips strained over big fangs. Moo Moo.

'Since you weren't there, Mabel, kindly let me talk to Seamus.'

'Well, dear, you're new here . . .'

'I'm not that new and I'm certainly not green, so . . .'

Seamus rose, gaunt and decaying. His tin limbs rattled inside the elegant pin-stripe suit and a stringy grey hand adjusted a ruby stickpin as he perforated my tongue with one lidless, tarnished eye. Thick, weightless bars of sun pushed the plaster walls of the tiny room until they buckled inwards, dirty windows swinging over the sagging sills. Identical plastic faces attached to identical bodies jammed together in a pudgy, fetid semi-circle around the star, who rasped.

'What are you doing here? Get back to your classes at once.' Whisky-laden air prodded my bruised ribs.

That was it. I had heard the end of today's incident. Nothing unpleasant was ever discussed with the individual involved. Dissension was hoarded, carefully preserved in a jar of pus, and presented on a diamond platter in a surreptitious staff meeting. Plastic faces donned disapproving expressions and condemned the absent loser. It was so easy to be brave and outspoken.

Seamus' private life and professional experience were shrouded in a fog of words, and our knowledge of him as a person was minimal. I had watched him teach the children occasionally, and found that he was an excellent teacher. As Headmaster, he kept the paper theatre drifting, in tension-drenched confusion, along its vacuous path to nowhere. The pus jar contained juicy details dredged from the private lives of his teachers and students, and the toxic odour of this festering scum pervaded the school, eliciting fear and strain. Occasionally the jar was shaken and Seamus would select, with a sterile scalpel, a fusty piece of information to be smeared on every blackboard. Motivations for his actions were an enigma. Rooted in his private life and personal problems, they bore no relation to the school which was under his control.

His greatest talent lay in the use of words. Fantastic lies were completely convincing as he twisted and warped well-seasoned facts into a mutable cloth-of-gold, suitable for wear by each member of his audiences. Facts, at St. Steven's, were tangible items to be altered according to the situation.

I stuck two cigarettes in my mouth and lit them. Mabel was bravely trying to smile at Seamus and me alternately. It was too difficult and she wrapped herself in a gauze adjective. Papier mâché masks replaced the sage expressions. There was, as yet, no winner and no loser.

I revolved down the corridor. Back to class.

CHAPTER TWO

'TODAY we have ten probation officers coming to visit us and I want you all to behave in a reasonably human fashion.'

We usually entertained visitors on Thursday. They formed the approving audience before whom Seamus performed with skill and enthusiasm, and included student teachers, education officers, parents and neighbours. Gathered in the dress-circle of Seamus' office they gaped in admiration and respect as Seamus fished in the pus box for a particularly putrid bit of information. Confidential files and reports were displayed for their perusal as Seamus entertained the stupefied groups, constructing evil pyramids of frothy words upon which he skipped and danced, directed and produced. Finale for the day's amusement was a tour of the school. Seamus carefully selected one student to escort each visitor through the school and around the grounds, vividly illustrating the remarkable improvements that had occurred during his tenure as Headmaster of a school for rejects. The visitors were impressed. Adolescents, excluded from every educational institution save the Borstals, had become coherent and presentable in this atmosphere. Graciously they conducted astonished guests over the grounds, lucidly explaining the transformations that Sir had wrought in this ancient building. It was now a real school. One with only nine classrooms for fourteen classes and a wealth of unused PT equipment rotting because there was no gym, workbenches without carpentry materials or instructor, and potters' wheels with no clay. No pencils and paper, no books. Sixteen-year-old students with a reading age of seven, unable to ride a bicycle because they could not decipher street signs. But there were numerous rat hutches, a pigeon coop, ducks, a goat, a donkey, a pair of (presumably female) grass snakes and a stoat, all cared for by the pupils. The animal pen had been built by the students, as well as the shed housing the caretaker's equipment. The wild murals on the exterior wall depicting animal scenes had been designed and painted by these violent adolescents.

The education officers went back to the board and wrote favourable reports, parents went home pacified, and teaching students were inspired and determined to enter special education.

'The law! The law!'

'Hey, Miss, is Mrs. Fraser coming? She's my probation officer.'

'Oi, twit-features! Mr. Green going to be around? I'm going home!'

A small plastic lady was on duty. She slipped on her teacher face.

'Will you kindly *shut up* so that we can say the prayer and dismiss assembly. Greta, put down the comic. Marrie, do not egg Gaylord on like that. You know ... *Gaylord*! If you stab Tina once more I'll smack you. Now give that compass to me a ... *don't throw it*! Naughty boy. Oh Tina, do shut up. Go to Mrs. Greely for a plaster. Marrie, if you ...'

Marrie jerked forth into action and warmed up for the day.

'You rotten old bitch. I wasn't doing nothing. Was I, Gaylord? Was I? It was Gaylord. Tell her, Gaylord, it was ...'

She trailed off, whispering to Gaylord who promptly darted after Tina, stabbing Mabel in the arm as he passed. Mabel screamed. Tina screamed and fled. Marrie's hysterical laughter spilled on to the front desk. Ray, Victor and Herbert held a farting contest in the back row. Nick turned on the transistor which he carried close to his navel at all times, and the only musical groin in the city produced the latest pop hit. Half a dozen students began stripping and dancing.

Silence unfolded from one end of the room to the other. Sir appeared in the doorway, treading on it, wrinkles painted mauve in the grey cartilage of his face. Fear pirouetted on forty shoulders as he strode into the closed room.

Fear doesn't smell, it stinks. It, mixed with the stench of forty unwashed bodies, several sewn up for the winter, putrid feet, and solid tears trapped in embalmed emotions. I gagged. Dense clouds of fermented odour spiralled around the carved cellophone figurines, crushing and compressing them into fluid cakes of diseased emotions and decayed nerves. The smell spread and lapped at the decrepit edges of the room. The appalling stench bleached the blackboard, extinguished the light, buckled the ceiling and trapped me in a cardboard box of frozen chloroform.

Wordless, Seamus picked up the nearest chair and sent it crashing into the school's sole bookcase. A door parted from its hinges, bowed and died with a splinter. He slammed a second chair on to the front desk. The chair was mortally wounded and the desk sustained a gaping, raw scar from one end to the other. The cloying stink of dead furniture mingled with the turbulent, offensive clouds of human fear, changing the room's odour from green to mottled red.

Seamus' voice grated through the hall, separating the odours into dripping elements.

'What is this? What's it all about? No one able to hear? I want an answer!' He faced mute, sculptured cellophane.

I leered at him through my false eyelashes, and blocked my ears with a blue brain. I watched my thoughts as they selected Seamus' favourite subject, 'control'.

'You can all have exactly the same degree and kind of control over these students that I have.'

No, I couldn't. Control he has, has had, will have: through fear and constant instability. Not fear of the cane, but fear of the police, Borstal, a boot on the bum, a call on the parents. Take a sick mind, add a few sick emotions, mould them into a box and wave an inch of fear in front. Watch the box sit, stand, kneel and laugh on order. Do I want control? I do not want control.

I unplugged my ears and my eyes focused on the jellied steel figure. He strolled between the ragged rows of students, giving an occasional kick to the backside, punch to the head, smack on the chops. I put on my blue-lensed sun glasses. Made for the summer sun in Aqaba they miraculously transformed the scene. My eyelashes dragged over an indigo fog, creating instant art. Adjust your television set. I took them off.

He undulated over to Gaylord who, through the magic power of fear, had scuttled back into the hall and now stood in a corner. Gaylord's back and legs were rigid, invertebrate blocks of waxed ebony, and his face was covered by bony, stiff fingers as he stood in his customary posture.

Seamus' hoarse voice scourged the cellophane packets.

'Now you know that Gaylord is just a naughty boy with an eight-year-old mind. Any one of you guilty of goading him is responsible for his actions. I don't want anyone to bully my boy Gaylord. And Gaylord, you want to go back to Guyana on the first banana boat?'

'No, Sir,' from behind the fists.

'Then leave my girl friend Tina alone.'

'Yes, Sir.'

Jesus, Mary, Joseph and all you lovely saints, do something. I looked at Una. She rolled her eyes, crossed herself and genuflected to Seamus.

Una, my only friend on the staff, had almost suffered a nervous breakdown last year. Her intolerable home life provided a poor environment for anyone in this type of work. School was, for her, a torment-studded anagram as Seamus goaded, jeered and gossiped about her West Indian background to sagely nodding balloons. During my initial interview with Seamus he had dipped into the pus pot for savoury details of Una's personal life, confiding to me that she was a neurotic cross which the school bravely bore. Regularly he spread the lurid scrollwork of her unhappy past before the staff for discussion and microscopic inspection. Outspoken, and completely honest, she struggled through the prickly network of gossip, always a loser.

Una was the best teacher I had ever known. She was onc of the few able to take a bit of wood, scrap of cloth or tube of cardboard, and concoct an absorbing craft or academic lesson. She adored the children and enveloped them in a warmth and security that they had never found elsewhere. At home she made dresses for the girls, collage pictures for the boys, and helped them all to remember family birthdays. She smacked them, loved them and taught well. In return, the children were devoted to her. Because she was an excellent teacher and a loser, Gaylord had been in her class for two years, and the interminable tension he generated was beginning to affect her physical and mental health.

It was evident to the entire staff that Gaylord was psychotic, not maladjusted, and should never have been placed in St. Steven's. Having once accepted the boy, and thus ruled him 'disturbed', Seamus adamantly refused to consider the possibility of any deeper psychological illness. He called a staff meeting and, on centre stage, burped up a greasy froth of persuasive words intended to dissuade us from our view. Receiving no applause and convincing no one, he became more melodramatic. It was his school and the staff meeting was over.

Gaylord threw a hatchet at Tina and we convened again. Una arrived laden with psychiatric reports and letters concerning the mental illness of the boy:

Psychiatric Report (Confidential) 1.2.1968

Gaylord began his interview as an apparently well adjusted Guyanese boy, but his anxiety and general neurosis very quickly surfaced. He would suddenly burst into wild, irrational laughter and when forced into direct answers would turn to the attack.

During both testing and interview, Gaylord was restless and distractible. Apparently bewildered by the questions asked, he either remained silent or gave vague, meaningless answers. The first test proceeded successfully with Gaylord in the co-operative spirit, but during subsequent testing it became obvious that no reliable estimate of the boy's intelligence was possible. Gaylord refused to attempt the Holborn Test.

Each question was answered identically: 'I don't know that yet,' or 'Let me think'. Exceedingly bizarre physical and verbal responses were elicited by the Block Design and Coding tests, while his answers on the Arithmetic tests were nonsensical. Throughout, the boy's responses were totally unrelated to the questions asked.

In my opinion, Gaylord is a disturbed adolescent of low intelligence. The overall result of testing indicates an extremely backward individual but I feel that he is incapable of relating to his surroundings and unwilling to co-operate. For example, I asked his age and address, the number of siblings at home and number of friends at school In reply to each question he responded, 'I don't know that yet.' Yet he said 'That's not my name' as I wrote his name on the Arithmetic Test.

Gaylord is reported to be quite troublesome at school and awkward at home. I believe he is an extremely disturbed boy and feel that he should be transferred to a psychiatric unit.

Patrick Fielding
Psychiatrist

The report described, in clinical language, Gaylord's present behaviour and responses at St. Steven's. In November a psychiatric social worker had written, on behalf of the educational psychologist, to a hospital on the coast, requesting that Gaylord be admitted for observation:

Dear Dr. Wisemann,

Following is further information regarding the boy Gaylord Silver, who is to be admitted tomorrow for observation. You will also find complete psychiatric reports and tests attached from which you can see that, as yet, no one has been able to determine the intelligence of this child.

Gaylord was referred to us in the spring of this year with a history of playing truant and absconding from school. During the time we have been in contact with him, the boy's behaviour has become increasingly bizarre and withdrawn.

Gaylord has attended school in Britain for the past six years and, until two years ago, was equal to his Guyanese contemporaries, albeit slightly backward. At that time Gaylord's large school underwent reorganization of groups and classes and we feel that this disturbance of his environment initiated the boy's present behaviour patterns. He was completely unable to establish contact with new staff and children in the school and, at that time, all academic progress halted.

Since last spring we have interviewed Gaylord eight times, during which he has been evasive and furtive. He grins, frowns and fidgets. Occasionally he hides his face behind his hands and refuses to communicate in any way. His speech is blurred and unintelligible and all questions are answered by 'I don't know that yet'.

Mrs. Silver restrains the boy by either locking him in a room or by taking his clothes away. She is unable to understand Gaylord's problems but has expressed definite antipathy to parting with her son for a prolonged period of time. She has agreed to this observation period but I can foresee difficulty with Mrs. Silver, should you find that extended treatment for Gaylord is necessary.

Gaylord is illegitimate and was left, for the first ten years of his life, with an aunt in Guyana. Mrs. Silver's movements at this time are unknown, but she arrived in England with four children and an African gentleman when Gaylord was almost ten years old. The boy was reunited with his mother shortly afterwards. Since that time Mrs. Silver has borne three more illegitimate children but has never achieved a permanent relationship with one man. She apparently has lived with a number of men since her arrival in this country, most of whom are impatient and intolerant of her children. Gaylord's own father is in Guyana and has had no contact with the boy for many years.

After Gaylord's first interview, we recommended admission to a day school for maladjusted children hoping that prolonged observation would occur. In such a case, resulting assessment of the boy's problems would be more accurate. Unfortunately there is no such school with a vacancy and, although we hope to place him as quickly as possible, his behaviour has now necessitated exclusion from his present school.

Mrs. Silver is employed and leaves Gaylord alone during the day. He is prone to wander even when his mother is at home and, on several occasions, has been returned at night by the police. Gaylord usually ventures out unclothed and, last week, appeared nude at his former school.

All authorities involved are concerned and considerably disturbed by this case and all are in agreement as to the great need of further observation. I should very much appreciate your help in the matter and look forward to receiving your report on the boy.

Yours sincerely,
R. Tanner

The result of the intensive examination was contained in a letter from the hospital dated one month later.

Dear Dr. Barns,

Dr. Wisemann has instructed me to write and report our findings regarding the boy Gaylord Silver, until recently under observation in the hospital.

Shortly after admission Gaylord absconded from the ward completely nude and unshod, thereby forcing us to transfer him to the closed ward. He remained in this location for the duration of his stay.

His behaviour in the hospital was consistently bizarre, deteriorated and solitary. He was unable to answer simple questions and, in fact, was verbally incapable of exhibiting relation to himself or his environment. We were unable to give him any tests by our Psychology Department due to the fact that, when approached, Gaylord hid under the bedclothes and refused to emerge. At mealtimes he stuffed food into his mouth by the handful, gorging himself with anything edible.

In our opinion it would appear that Gaylord suffers from a definite psychosis.

Yours sincerely,
S. Taylor
Senior Registrar

Gaylord had then been accepted as a student at St. Steven's. During his first days at school he crammed food into his mouth with both hands, licking the plate, scratching his head, scratching his bottom, caking food on his face, on the chair, on the table and on the floor. Often he ate seven or eight lunches during the school day. After this initial gluttony, food was withheld until he ate properly and, not surprisingly, he quickly learned to use acceptable table manners. Almost mute when he arrived, Gaylord had learned to converse in a limited manner over the past two years, but he had also become uncontrollably violent. In an instant and without warning he could turn on the nearest bystander and stab, slash and crush. The only check was fear of greater violence.

The staff, for once, consolidated. We were all afraid of Gaylord. We were not trained for work with the insane.

Staff meetings were endless, eternal and useless. The subject was Gaylord.

'Where can we send him if he doesn't stay with us? If we exclude him, his mother will lock him in at home. I can't have that.'

I rang a psychiatrist, explained the problem, and asked which institutions would take a psychotic boy of sixteen years. That afternoon I gave Seamus the names of two mental hospitals that admit adolescents and give psychiatric treatment, social therapy and vocational training.

'They won't take Gaylord. He's sixteen.'

'They take sixteen-year-olds, Seamus.'

'They won't take Gaylord.'

What's the use!

The children's officer submitted Gaylord's name for entry in a local institution. Seamus hooked his shining gold charm over one decayed fang, summoned Gaylord's mother to school and persuaded her to refuse permission. Without the mother's consent it was almost impossible to commit the boy to any residential institution, and we still had Gaylord. The children's officer paid a visit to school, begging Seamus to stop 'rocking the boat'. He polished his charm, oiled a few frothing words, and escorted the officer around the school. A personally conducted tour over the antiseptic stage to view the props which were displayed in hygienic medicinal packets. Inhaling the healthful, disinfectant air that permeated St. Steven's, the children's officer departed. Seamus examined his charm for defects. We still had Gaylord.

'Seamus, why don't you want him to go to Millward?'

'They use drugs.'

'They prescribe drugs as part of the treatment.'

I thought wistfully of the calming drugs that were administered to psychotics in the institution.

'I don't want Gaylord to become a junkie.'

'Oh my God, Seamus, you don't want him to become anything.'

'It isn't necessary to turn him into a vegetable.'

'You aren't listening, Seamus, he is a vegetable.'

'They won't take Gaylord.'

'Seamus, the officer was here because they have a vacancy for Gaylord, if you'll just let him go.'

'They won't take him.'

Although Seamus refused to admit it, even to himself, he could not release Gaylord. The boy was a necessary prop on the turbulent stage, a vital support to Seamus' star role in the inconstant production at St. Steven's. Seamus visualized himself starring as 'The Mind Mender', achieving Gaylord's rehabilitation in a brilliant solo performance. The tattered mind would be neatly mended with a decorative satin stick, the vacant eyes would sparkle and radiate sanity, and the boy would stride forth from St. Steven's, a well-adjusted, contributing member of society.

In this special school for maladjusted children there was no one qualified to give psychiatric help to any of the students, and certainly no one capable of treating a demented child. We contained the children and, if we were blest with an extraordinary combination of talent and luck, we also taught, but none of us were trained to explore the sticky quagmire of problems that determined the overt behaviour of each child. We had once been assigned an excellent psychiatric social worker who visited the homes of our students, dealt with parents, wrote psychological reports and recommended various forms of treatment for the disturbed adolescents. Unfortunately, she was thoroughly trained in her profession and insisted upon administering necessary tests and treatment. Seamus found that he was unable to direct the play alone and that, from time to time, he was appearing behind the floodlights with a fellow actor of equal standing. In an inspired enactment, he told us that we were dispensable marionettes. All of us. It was his school. The psychiatric social worker was dismissed after six months, and we floundered through the morass of violence, tension and problems without trained help.

Seamus produced the charade, and we dealt with Gaylord. One psychotic in a class of ten maladjusted students produces one unbalanced teacher.

The staff meetings went on. And on. And on.

'Psychotic? What do you mean psychotic? Show me your degrees in psychology and then I'll think about it.'

My eyes were on stalks, shaded by black false lashes. They rotated through the room and swept the mud over his polished shoes. The mauve wrinkles turned to ochre. I am the only one on the staff with any degree and mine is in psychology. He bowed and swept the mud over my soleless shoes. Forget it.

He wanted us to agree that he was right. His judgement was infallible. We refused, he tried. We refused, he tried. The charm that had convinced education officers, parents and students clicked on. We clicked it off. He tried. We refused. We still have endless staff meetings. About Gaylord. Gaylord is still with us. And he will be here until he is seventy-four years old. He will still be uncontrollable and we will still quake in fear – and have breakdowns.

'Now go to your classes and act like humans if you can.' I revolved down the corridor. To class.

CHAPTER THREE

My class was seated and relatively quiet. Boysie was stoned again, staring at the wall, eyes sleeping in a knuckle-duster. He had begun to smoke hash in the showers. I knew it and I refused to tell Seamus. Sir would summon the boy backstage and entomb him in a suffocating envelope of sticky lectures, spiky threats and oiled pleas, this eliciting rancid information for the pus pot. My class would bestow an 'Animosity Award' on me. It would serve no purpose to hand Sir the puzzle in a cubed postage stamp. Boysie would continue to smoke pot in the loo, dealing with an insoluble problem in his own unique manner. He was lacing himself into hash armour with a Purple Heart shield. I plaited my nerves and brushed the desk with the fringed edges. Boysie stared at a snow white wall.

I had asked him, not long ago:

'What's the point, Boysie? You've no business fooling around with drugs. You know what can happen, you've seen it often enough.'

'Yeah, but I'm happy for a while, ain't I?'

'Oh sure, and when you come down again you have the same problem. It doesn't go away, you know.'

'Well, I ain't gotta think about it so much, do I?'

My lessons were planned to interest Boysie, Stewart and Marrie. If they were captivated by the knowledge I offered they worked and forced the rest of the class to study. If these three were bored I might as well pack it in for the day. Astronomy and zoology were favoured subjects and my mind bent and touched toes.

My relationship with Boysie evolved through time, genuine affection and patience. He had once told me,

'You're the only teacher what I've done nothing for.

Anything for. Hang about, I mean I do what you want me to do. I told the others to fuck off.'

He had once told me the same thing in specific terms. The first class I had been assigned at St. Steven's was composed of 'uncontrollables'. Boysie greeted me on the first day.

'I don't like you.'

'That's too bad because I like you.'

This was, apparently, a stopper. He was silent for over an hour.

'Oi, you. Why dontcha learn to speak properly?' A blast of stinging slang spewed over the teacher's desk as my mind unreeled across the blackboard to understand. It reeled in again with a translation.

'Like maybe you should teach me,' – in garbled Bronx.

Following this intellectual repartee he began sitting on the radiator, which was forbidden. He slept through class. I slung clotted wisdom at his inert peers, diagramming a sentence through raucous snores.

He slumped against the piano, bum comfortably resting on the puffing radiator. Brown eyes were, as usual, firmly closed against any foreign thoughts as I began my daily lecture.

'The sun is composed of millions of atoms, crushed together by tons of pressure. These atoms are so tightly packed that they split into pieces. When the nucleus, or centre, of an atom breaks, one of the pieces turns into a huge light, heat and energy. An example is the atom bomb.'

Black motorcycle boots, the wearing of which was forbidden in class, bombarded the aged floor and Boysie's eyes flicked open.

'Bomb?'

'Yes, bomb.'

'Like a normal bomb?'

'Well, um, more or less . . . yes.'

'Well I can make a bomb. I fucking blew up a car with one last weekend.'

'You mean you *made* the bomb?'

'Yeah, where else'd I get a bomb?'

'How should I know? Can you make one now?'

'Yeah. Yeah. You mean *here*?

'Of course I mean here. I want you to conduct a class demonstration.' One picture is worth a million words and one home-made bomb reconditions and cleans several disintegrated personalities.

'What do you need?'

'Fucking hell, just weed-killer and sugar. Oh yeah, some copper tubing, but I've got that myself.'

He pulled an assortment of tubes from his jacket pocket, along with a pair of knuckledusters, three condoms and two pennies. Life's necessities.

'Well hurry and get the sugar and weed-killer.'

I watched the plastic faces watching me. I would be a winner today.

Boysie mixed the sugar and weed-killer, filled a small tube and stuffed the end with paper. He had had a lot of practice, sometime. The end of the copper was hammered shut.

'Can I light it here?'

'*In the classroom?* Good God, of course not.'

Our class drifted to a clearing behind the school on a weed-killer cloud. The bomb was borne on a wad of mangled black hair while one hundred masks were held aloft over one hundred cream-cheese faces.

'Now save some of the mixture and pour it in a heap. I want you to see the difference between atoms crushed and exploding and atoms burning unencumbered.'

'Yes, Miss,' one hundred times.

Awe and respect from the class as Boysie arranged the bomb with a trail of weed-killer-sugar leading to it. Eight students, one hundred masks and five saints watched. The latter would, I presumed, protect the students as they executed an Iroquois war dance over the waiting bomb.

'Get *back*, you stupid fools. I don't want to go hunting in the autumn grass for any fingers or bosoms.'

Eight ha-has.

Fire sped along the trail of powder. The explosion was tremendous and brought cherubic smiles to my class. It also brought down a small tree, brought out a wrathful Headmaster and five staff members. They were wearing masks of disapproval and holding sixteen more each. Una wore her own face. I wore mine. With my false eyelashes.

'Class demonstration,' I called, waving the eyelashes.

The remainder of the week passed in cheerful bomb-making and exploding. The class was gleeful. The staff gloomy.

Friday.

'Now class, we've seen how atoms work. Let's not hear of any Mad Bombers terrorizing the countryside over the weekend. Try and have fun anyway and stay out of the nick.'

I've never had trouble with Boysie since. No one has made a bomb since either. In or out of school.

CHAPTER FOUR

BOYSIE had never learned to read or write past a seven-year level, although his IQ was 116. He set high standards for himself which, because he lacked fundamental skills, were unattainable. Taking refuge in belligerence he fell further and further behind his classmates in academic accomplishment while his standards rose. He dreamed of composing perfect prose but knew in advance that failure was insured, so he told each teacher,

'Fuck off.'

He was sent to the Head for the cane, returned to class and said,

'Fuck off, I still won't do it.'

He was sent out to stand under the clock. He had spent months of his life standing under various school clocks, but no one, until he came to St. Steven's, had been concerned enough to discover that he was unable to tell the time. Seamus taught him, at the age of eleven, that a clock indicated more than a means of punishment. Like most of the children at school, no one had been really interested in Boysie. No one knew his abilities, his limitations, his problems or his desires. He was a delinquent, an obstruction, a cross to bear. He was sent to us.

Boysie's parents were working-class, non-smoking, non-drinking Cape-coloured Bible-thumpers who were stunned and nonplussed by the behaviour of this particular progeny. Envisioning a plodding, unspectacular progress through school to the factory by each of their eleven children, they tried to curb Boysie's racking probe into life and experience through a volley of gospel-based pleas. He plugged his ears with rice, jammed a Purple Heart into his pocket and jumped on to Desmond's motorbike to look for answers.

After a week of bomb-building, my class settled to the arduous task of learning to spell, compose and think, regarding me as a slightly mad character in the poorly written novel Life, and hoping for more lively class demonstrations. The mountain of knowledge was adorned with sharpened drawing pins, and it often took more than an hour of protest, obscene banter and prolonged setting up exercises before the faces were turned, silent and resigned, to receive the wisdom I spun in a glass yo-yo. Improvement was tortuous and sluggish but measurable. Gradually they accepted the fact that I was begging cooperation and should they refuse I would be disappointed, not vindictive. Having spent the first weeks trying ineffectually to shock me, they next established the limit of my tolerance with the assistance of Barbara, our school goat. This demarcation line firmly drawn in curdled nerve endings, they took out pencils and papers, belched loudly and composed.

Reminding myself that my charges were rejected, unloved and disturbed, I had ploughed through a maelstrom of foul language and outrageous behaviour without losing my temper until we took Barbara for a walk. As a kid, Barbara had been forcibly removed from a farmyard by Timmy, who took her home and secreted her in his bed. The head of the household was understandably concerned when he discovered that his youngest son was sleeping with a goat, and St. Steven's adopted the homeless animal.

The children adored Barbara and, as a reward for an hour of reasonably sane behaviour, they were frequently allowed to walk in the park, accompanied by Barbara and a teacher. Six weeks after school began I decided that my class deserved this rare treat.

We assembled in front of the school with Stewart and Eddy restraining Barbara on a chain lead. At the signal my class charged out the gate and galloped down the street towards the park. Lorries braked to a stop, housewives hid tiny children behind sagging skirts, and shopkeepers turned to stare through windows filled with plastic buckets and bronze frying-pans as we pelted along the pavement behind the goat.

'Marrie, don't ride on Barbara, please.'

'Fuck off, you old bitch.'

Mothers blocked their children's ears and elderly gentlemen clutched quivering canes for support as we brushed past, the children screaming and knocking obstructions from the path.

'Will you please slow down.' I screeched, panting in my efforts to keep within earshot. 'You must behave in a better fashion than you do at school or we will have no more excursions.'

'Shove it up your ass.' A shopkeeper slammed his door.

'We're going to the fucking park, ain't we? We won't bloody get there if we slow down.'

'Come on, Barbara, run.'

Stewart snapped the goat's jouncing backside and she reared up on her hind legs. A mother screamed and propelled her pram towards the local police station. Barbara reared again, dropped to all fours, and lowered her head. Unfortunately, a greengrocer was arranging a pavement display case of apples and his broad bum presented an irresistible target. She pawed the ground and butted the gentleman, lifting him high above the waxy green fruit. As he dropped to the cement Barbara caught his jacket, ripping a large chunk from the back and, tweed streaming from the corners of her mouth, galloped off towards the park, dragging Eddy and Stewart. The students screamed with mirth and stormed down the street in the goat's wake.

'Fucking hell. Did you see that old git?'

'Come on, Barbara, chew!'

'Gi'us a bite, Barb.'

'Come on, *run*!'

I stopped by the greengrocer who now sprawled over a heap of apples.

'Please let me help you up. I'm so sorry about his. I'm really dreadfully embarrassed over our goat's behaviour. She's maladjusted, you know. I mean, the students are from the maladjusted school, and it's very difficult at times.'

I heaved him to a standing position, and he crammed spectacles on to a bulbous red nose. Removing his jacket, he surveyed the damage. The entire back was missing.

'Who're you?'

'I'm the teacher in charge of the group.'

'You don't look like a teacher to me.' He glared suspiciously at my long false lashes and snuffled in obvious distaste after a quick peep at my very short mini skirt. 'What's the name of that school? Look at my coat. Ruined. What's the matter with those kids? They mad or something? I've got a boy meself and if he acted like those maniacs I'd belt him one. That's what all those kids need. A bloody good belting.' I saw the class disappear, screaming, into the wooded park:

'I really must go and look after the class. St. Steven's is the school. I'm sure you know of it. I'm dreadfully sorry about the coat but these children are very trying at times.'

I left him apoplectic and green-hued, surrounded by great mounds of bruised fruit and sped down the road in search of my class.

There was no sign of any student as I entered the wood. Sun-drops sifted through a netting of oak leaves, and fell on damp, mottled earth. Fallen logs, overgrown by grass and brambles, sheltered beneath massive thickets, and the moss which clung to the twisted tree trunks exuded the smell of wet decay. Sound was muffled in the damp, green velvet. I could hear the growth of small insects as they pushed through the matted foliage and splattered on the spongy vegetation.

'Marrie! Victor! John! All of you, come here this instant!'

Barbara jumped over a log, butted me in the rear, and I fell, enveloped by a froth of moss and decaying leaves. Pulling myself upright, I took the dragging chain lead and began pawing through the tangled bushes in search of my class. I fell over Marrie smoking beneath a large shrub.

'Put that cigarette out at once and come with me. The class is supposed to stay together and behave in an exemplary manner when we leave the school grounds, as you well know. If this is your idea of proper behaviour, I promise you we will have no more excursions this year.'

'Why don't you fuck off.'

She rose, clumps of brown earth and rotting vegetation

clinging to her shabby skirt, and ground out the cigarette.

'Gimme that goat. Barbara likes me, dontcha Barb?'

She leaned down to pat Barbara just as a spluttering object flashed over her head and exploded in a blaze of light. I stared at the spitting firecracker on the ground and my head expanded, filling with a green lump of fear. My throat constricted over a crate of frustration and rage as I quickly counted the beads on my nerves.

Stewart, Victor and John were perched in a tree, grinning down at us.

'You stupid, idiotic fools! Get out of that tree at once. What in the hell do you think you're doing? If Marrie hadn't bent down that firecracker would have put out her eye. You haven't got the sense God gave a maggot.'

'You just fuck off, you big moo. Wait'll I tell my Dad.' Marrie's eyes jiggled in liquid fear.

'We are all going back to school *now* and the three of you will *not* come to Bonfire Night. You have just had your firecrackers for the year.'

Smiles faded as they swung down from the tree.

'Shit, Miss, I've never seen you cross before.'

'We was just joking.'

'Shut up and move along. We will not have any more excursions this term either.'

'What about the rest of the class?'

'If they can't stay with us they can rot in this wood. I'm not chasing around the park for anyone else.'

I stamped back to the High Street, followed by Marrie and the goat. The three boys scuffed disconsolately in the rear. When we reached the houses adjoining the school Marrie began picking roses from front gardens and feeding them to Barbara.

'Stop it, Marrie, those aren't your flowers.'

'Fuck that.' She ripped up a small rose bush and shoved it into Barbara's mouth. A man straightened up from his garden, hoe in hand, and shouted. Marrie slapped the goat to a trot and began to pull fistfuls of flowers from gardens as they passed. When Barbara's mouth was crammed, she pushed the blooms into her own mouth, shrilling between gulps of petals,

'Come on, Barb, faster.'

From every house and garden men and women appeared, shouting at Marrie, who screamed back over her shoulder.

'Fuck off, you sods.'

The irate neighbours stopped shouting and trotted to the pavement. The boys stopped dawdling and began to run, pursued by a score of rose-bush owners. I ran. Barbara and Marrie thundered up the drive to school, mouths stuffed with flowers, leading a procession of students, teacher and neighbours.

Seamus was standing on the front step toying with his large gold watch. The greengrocer, torn coat dangling from his plump hand, didn't pause in the conversation as we screeched to a stop.

'Now, Mr. O'Shea, I understand the situation perfectly. You have me sympathy. Blimey. I couldn't cope with these maniacs. I take off me cap to you for trying to do anything with them. I think you're very brave.' He glared at me.

Seamus peered and bestowed an oily smile on the greengrocer.

'I'm glad you understand my problem, Mr. Stoner. We try and keep up good relations with the townspeople. Marrie, *take those flowers out of your mouth*! Goodbye then, Mr. Stoner. Drop in any time at all. I'll have one of the boys take you around the school and show you what we do here.'

Mr. Stoner recoiled in horror at the thought.

'Oh no, I couldn't put you out. Lovely to talk to a Headmaster like you, though.' They shook hands and a pacified Mr. Stoner strolled out of the gate, almost trampled by the angry neighbours who surged past him on the way in.

'Now, *what is this?*'

White liver spots appeared, and blotched the green complexion as his tiny joints began to rattle in fury.

'Marrie's eaten the neighbours' flowers, the boys almost put her eye out with a firecracker, the rest of the class is lost in the park, Barbara ate the greengrocer's coat, and I'm sorry. I'll see you about it later.'

I pivoted on gangrenous toes and whirled to the back of the school to sit under a tree. Leaves flaked into dried tears and squashed my right cheek. Sunlight squeezing through the foliage pressed my brain into a soggy pancake spread with rose-hip jelly, as the malformed orange triangle in the sky jerked down towards the horizon. Marrie crept around the tree.

'Sorry, Miss. We didn't mean to get you in trouble.'

'It's all right, Marrie, but there still will be no more excursions and no Bonfire night.'

'I gotta go apologize to those pissy neighbours. They're just spiteful.' She coughed and then sat in silence. 'You wouldn't wanna come with me 'n' tell me whatta say to the old sods?'

'Yes, I'll go with you. Come on.'

'*Now?* Fucking hell!'

'If we're going to do it we'll do it now. Coming?'

We got up and trudged towards the gate. My mind squeaked and leaped on to the roulette wheel. Number thirteen.

'All right, get out your pencils and paper.'

'Aw.'

'Writing again. All we do is write in here.'

'Shitty old school.'

'Will you shut up and do as I say, please. I'm going to write a title on the board and you will write a composition on that theme. Remember, whatever this title brings to mind will be your theme.'

'What's a theme?'

I wrote 'The Man' on the board.

'Who's that?'

'What man?'

'You talking about Sir?'

'I *said* this will mean different things to different people, so write upon your own theme. This is *supposed* to make you think.'

'That's too hard.'

'Oi, can't I write about Timmy? He went nicking last night.'

'You're an old cow.'

I batted false, black lashes.

'I'm what?'

'Well, you're not old, but you're a cow.'

'I hate teachers.'

'So hate teachers, but shut up and get busy. You must do this before break, so you don't have much time.'

I sat on my desk and tuned up my nerves. Rare silence filled the room, broken only by the sound of delinquent minds munching on lined paper. I never sat at my desk, or behind it or beside it. I was right on top where I could uncoil one of my nine arms and batter trouble to death. Trouble was for ever hiding in an undetected mouse-hole, awaiting the opportunity to emerge, and it would never trap me behind a desk.

Ten probation officers strolled past the window on their way to the front door as I counted the ladders in my stockings. Seven, one of them huge. Pencils tapped in frustration, brows furrowed, and lips moved slowly, as unused brains were set painfully in motion. Seamus' voice grated through the school, summoning the escorts. Only Boysie was called out from my class. He sat, unhearing and unmoving.

Stewart held up a paper for Marrie to see, then crumpled it and collapsed across his desk with burping laughter. Marrie's legs and mouth moved simultaneously. I jumped off the desk and ran to push her back into the chair while she screeched:

'You wait, Stewart Robertson, I'll beat your fucking head in.'

I didn't know about Stewart but I was convinced. She had been on probation four times and once the charge was assault. She used her fists to cope with all problems, irrespective of time or place.

Behind me I heard Stewart break into snorted fits of laughter as he shredded the offensive paper into tiny bits.

Marrie poked her head around me, twisting her face and neck into stringy cords.

'You'll be sorry for that, Stew . . .'

I shoved her down into the chair and raised my voice.

'Stewart and Marrie! I want this to stop *now* or I'll have you both after school. Now write your compositions.'

God. Enter trouble with lilies and barbed wire. Where was the mouse-hole today? I took out one of my nerves and examined it. Looked all right.

Stewart held up another paper for Marrie. Skinny legs dug at the floor as she pushed backwards and flung up the desk top, screaming,

'Fuck off, you rotten sod, you can just piss off.'

She began to sling pencils, books and ink from the desk's interior across the room at Stewart. The classroom door edged open and, through the barrage of flying objects and shrieks of abuse, the probation officers and their escorts entered.

'Fuck off, you old cunt. You pissy-arsed bastard.'

A bottle of ink hit the wall and sprayed a visiting grey-flannel suit with permanent black stain. I advanced towards the well-dressed group who, with stunned faces, were beholding maladjustment in action. Stewart ducked as a handful of coloured pencils shot across the room at his head.

'Good morning. I'm Miss MacMichael and this is my class. Today we are writing a composition entitled "The Man".'

'Fuck off, you just fuck off . . .'

Stewart shook with laughter and stamped workman's boots on the floor. A flying pen struck his ear and he ducked again, still laughing.

'You can fuck off, Stew, fuck off . . .'

The officers began to edge back towards the door.

Boysie's eyes dripped from an acid windowpane.

CHAPTER FIVE

BREAK. I was on duty and my services were required in ineffectual surveillance of the school grounds. Staff coats and wellingtons were currently kept in Seamus' office wardrobe and I reeled down the corridor in that direction, pushing through a packed mass of screaming, brawling students. As I reached the door Gaylord picked a fish from the tank, threw it at Tina, and was rewarded by an ear-splitting cackle from Marrie.

'That's it, Gaylord! Get that big fish! Come on, Gay, get 'em all . . .'

I turned the knob and tried to push the door open. It was jammed. I pushed harder, swung one hip against the door and found myself propelled across the office as the door was suddenly released.

Flattened against the far wall, I clutched at the nearest chair for support, dug my soleless shoes into the wooden floor and probed my head for any possible skull fracture. The curtains had been drawn and the room was in darkness. Focusing through the gloom I peered at a tall figure who was, apparently, struggling to button his trousers. I leaned forward.

'Who is that? Who drew these curtains? Open them at once!' I fervently hoped that the gaunt figure was not that of Seamus, abruptly caught in some forbidden game in his own office.

I was ignored. The battle with the trousers continued with increasing frenzy and, jerked into action, I threw open the nearest curtains. Stunned by the sudden glare of light, Abel stopped struggling with his fly. He stood motionless for a moment, then peeped guiltily at me.

'Oi, Miss.'

My head throbbed from the blow, my eyes bulged and I felt my ability to cope slipping rapidly. Pushing myself to an upright, dignified position I located my voice and directed it across the room.

'For God's sake, what *are* you doing in here with your trousers down? This is out of bounds to the students for a start, and you damned well know it! Will you be so kind as to answer me now?'

Still motionless, Abel stood with head dangling. I became vaguely aware of a movement on the floor behind the desk and took a few tentative steps in that direction. The entire room jolted into frantic, frenzied activity. Abel wrestled with the final button, adjusted his trousers and began stuffing his grimy shirt into tattered blue jeans. Behind the desk there was a violent thrashing. The wall thudded, Seamus' chair vibrated, and the floor was repeatedly smacked. As I sped around the desk I was jerked to a halt by the sight of Nonda. Lying on the floor, dress up to her neck, she was attempting to pull on a pair of very grey knickers. They were, apparently, stuck around her knees and now, red-faced, she flailed the air, wall and furniture with her feet. Hips rocking, she pulled viciously at the unco-operative underpants. I peered down at her. She flopped into motionless silence and, as belligerently as was possible from a half-nude, spread-eagle position on the floor, glared back at me. Outside in the corridor I could hear shrieks and screams as Gaylord, encouraged by Marrie, continued to capture the residents of our tiny aquarium and pelt the student body with his prey.

I straightened, arranged my dignity, and asked an inane question.

'Just *what* are you two doing?'

The answer was obvious. Both students were silent.

'Get up off that floor at once, Nonda, and explain this behaviour to me.'

Abel's head lolled, his hands were jammed into his jeans and he stared raptly at the aged floor. Nonda jumped up, hauled the knickers into place and pulled down her dress. Grunting slightly, she bent and fished a pair of mauve, spike-heeled summer sandals from under Seamus' desk and slid them on to her unwashed feet. Curving her hands into claws, she vainly attempted to comb out the tangles in her greasy, black hair. Abandoning any such effort, she folded her hands, dropped her head and gazed at the wet spot in front of the door.

'You ain't gonna tell Sir, are ya, Miss? We was just having a little fun.'

I stared at her.

'Having a *little fun*? In here? In Seamus' *office*?'

Abel's head jerked up and his voice broke to a tin squeak.

'Well we ain't got no other place to have it off, do we?'

'Haven't any other place?'

'That's what I said, Miss. Weren't no one in here. Fuck. How'd we know you'd come poking around here?'

I sighed. My head was filled with jangling nerves and I wished myself anywhere else.

'Of course I'm going to tell Sir. This is his office, in case you are not aware of the fact. You fail to realize that he, or any other of the staff, could have been the one to fall over you two.'

'Well they didn't, did they? S'truth! It ain't like it was something new, is it?'

'This is still one of those things that I must report to Sir. I'm sorry, I don't want to, but I must and you both understand it perfectly well. Now get back to your classrooms.'

Abel slunk out of the office, hands in pockets, while Nonda pranced away adjusting her matted hair.

'Slag,' hissed Abel from one corner of his mouth.

'Piss off, you dirty sod,' she returned primly. Head high and disdainful she minced off in the direction of her classroom.

Sighing once more I probed at my scalp. I was rewarded by renewed throbbing. Fearfully I set off in search of Seamus.

Unfortunately I found him just outside the front door. More unfortunate still, he was in a singularly bad humour. As I related the story he coiled around the water tap, mechanically twisting his signet ring. The mauve wrinkles deepened in the parchment skin, and the grey hoods dropped over his eyes.

'*My office? My office?* Jesus! You were on duty. It's your responsibility! My God, the staff I have in this dump. I can control these kids with one hand behind me and you can't even keep them from fucking in *my office*. What if Nonda's in the pudding club? Uh? How's that going to sound to her parents? Impregnated in *Mr. O'Shea's Office*! In school hours. In *my office*! I want to see both of them, and the rest of the staff, in that office right now!'

He slithered off to the contaminated room and I reeled away to summon the rest of the staff.

The staff sat on chairs jammed into Seamus' office. Abel fidgeted in the centre, head down, hands in pockets. Alternately bending his knees, he shuffled from one sock-clad foot to the other, occasionally kicking at a piece of invisible dust with one big toe. Both socks were matted with the grime of several months and riddled with holes of various sizes. His toenails, uncut, curled over black toes. Evidently the socks and feet were laundered together.

Identical expressions of vicarious enjoyment were plastered on the balloons as they fired questions at the boy in well-modulated tones. His voice broke to a squeak as he answered.

'Well she wanted me to.'

'How many times have you had, uh . . . um, sexual intercourse with your friend Nonda?'

'Had what?' The head lolled to one side and his eyes peered warily at his interrogator.

'Sexual intercourse. Surely you know what that means.'

'Oh yeah. Sex. Fucking hell, ya must think I'm stupid.'

'That doesn't answer the question that I asked. My opinon of you is well known.' Muted giggles of appreciation at this witticism were heard from the assembled staff. 'How many times?'

'Oh sod it, I don't know, do I?' Abel rocked from side to side, scratching his head in concentration. 'Ten or twenty. Something like that. Bollocks! How'm I supposed to remember something like that?' He twitched one slouched shoulder in indignation.

The staff members leaned forward in fascination.

'Ten or twenty? In *here*?'

'Christ's sake no! S'truth.' He chuckled nervously.

'Well then, *where*?'

'Oh, I dunno. In the loo or the cloakroom.' His scabrous scalp puckered in concentration. 'In the Black Swan parking lot. Most times in the shack.'

Stunned silence descended, broken by Seamus' thunderous voice.

'*What* shack?'

Abel looked at him in astonishment. 'The one we built under that tree in the park. We had it for ever so long, haven't we? It's only a place to go for a piece of slag like when it's raining.'

Seamus rose from his chair and began to dance around the boy. He pirouetted and slithered, ashen-faced, around the boy who, in turn, shuffled more rapidly in order to face the Headmaster at all times. All students in St. Steven's were wise enough to face Seamus when he was in such a mood. A slap to the face or blow on the shoulder was preferable to a boot on the bottom or a punch in the kidneys.

'Who's *"we"*? What *"slags"*?'

Gaunt, emaciated, Seamus once more dominated the stage.

'All the geezers except the moos.' Abel snorted loudly. 'All they want is a wank in the loo. All us gits and Nonda and Bernie, Frieda ... um, sometimes the Black Swan slags. Dunno who else.'

The cords in Seamus' neck worked feverishly.

'You go there all together?'

'Yeah, sometimes. Fucking hell, why not? Ain't nothing else to do, is there?'

'You have sexual intercourse there all together? Several at a time?'

'Yeah, why not?'

'How often?'

'Dunno. Whenever we feel like it.'

'Is this in school time?'

Abel emitted a coarse bellow, recognized by all present as his normal form of laughter, which was quickly strangled by the sight of Seamus' mottled face.

'Fucking hell, Sir, we can't get to the park during school hours. We go around teatime I guess.'

Seamus danced in silence. Abel, head down, shuffled in response. Seamus' voice, low and hoarse, spewed venom at the boy.

'You remember this, Abel. The next time you do one thing wrong at this school, the *next time*, your father is going to get a letter from me about this abominable behaviour. Seducing girls! God. You are about the most disgusting boy I've ever allowed to stay in this place. Now I want you to get *out* and get home. And remember, the next thing wrong I'll have your arse on a plate. Now *get out*!'

Humped over in half-moon shape, Abel slunk from

the office. Seamus, pulling out his gold pocket watch, took centre stage.

'We've taken almost forty minutes over this crap. That means forty minutes added to the end of the school day. If you weren't so damned inefficient, Conor, this would never have happened.' They beamed happily. 'Now Mabel, get that girl down for a pregnancy test.'

Mabel stretched fat lips over her protuding fangs and reached efficiently for a pad of paper and pencil. Writing rapidly, she jotted notes to herself, then turned expectantly towards Seamus.

'Now we'll all say a few prayers to Buddha, that she's not in the club. I want those loos and cloakrooms patrolled constantly and this office door to be kept locked. What they do outside school is no concern of mine, but what they do here in *my* school is my responsibility. I *will not* explain to any parents that their daughter became pregnant in MY OFFICE. Now get back to your classes and if any of you let this come out in gossip outside these four walls I will crucify you.'

We filed out of the sacred room. We went back to our classes. Mabel took Nonda for her test and it was returned with a negative report. Everyone was relieved and the staff happy. It was all right – but not in Seamus' office.

CHAPTER SIX

It was three a.m. Three hundred a.m. Two thousand and thirty-three on Jupiter. I must find my head and my contact lenses.

Outside my flat in a prim area of the town I could hear motorcycles roaring up and down the street, stopping, revving, living, dying, screaming. The doorbell, and then hammering on the door with something that sounded suspiciously like knuckledusters. I shuffled out of bed and put on a coat, I shuffled back into bed, closed my eyes and the lids fell into a motorcycle helmet.

Good God. I heard the cultured voice of Mr. Sears, ex-army officer, chief accountant, bachelor, boring bastard, and resident of the downstairs flat.

'Now I say, I'm going to call the police and have you all arrested for disturbing the peace. I won't have this going on. Have you any idea of the time?'

'Fuck off, you old git. I didn't come here to see you.'

Boysie. I struggled to find the floor, failed, and rode out through the keyhole on a contact lens. I wish I could go to Greece. Right now. If I teach loyally and faithfully for the next thirty years and save my sixpences I can go. On an economy coach. I'm freezing to death and the stairs are lost somewhere.

'Never mind, Mr. Sears, it's one of my students to see me. I'm coming.'

I was unable to locate the staircase so I selected the most beautiful fireman's pole and slid down.

The city's most respectable accountant pulled viciously at the lapels of his tartan dressing-gown in an attempt to modulate the tone of his upper-class accent. Spittle showered the opaque eyes of my visitor as Mr. Sears vomited, in a dry heave, the hemlock of a withered soul.

'Shameful! Shameful! Damned disgusting. Young idiots. You must all be mad. Have you no pride? Look at yourselves. You should all be locked away and given a good caning. This has always been a respectable residence and now look. I'm appalled by such a dreadful spectacle. I shall speak to the landlady tomorrow who, by the way, is a very dear friend of mine. I will not tolerate this type of behaviour.'

He tugged at a sword displayed on the wall and, backing against the door, flailed the air in our direction with the ancient weapon. I stared at the twisting figure who, with a contorted face and spittle streaming from his mouth, leaped and danced in the gloom. My memory walked backward through the chicken-wire maze towards the time when I had gone to theatres and dinner parties, my belly never had a nervous twitch, and the cellophane people wore eiderdown skins. The maze turned into a slime circle and fell upside down into the snow.

The hallway was embroidered with trophies of Mr. Sears' army career, Swords, photographs and purloined Indian treasures, tenderly polished and dusted, hung on the musty wall. Two large porcelain jars balanced on a waxed windowledge beside an enormous, frayed tapestry of indeterminate colours. Just inside the front door a massive concave brass gong, ornately engraved in a pattern of Asian flowers and birds, reposed in sterile elegance upon a carved rosewood frame. Each evening Mr. Sears knelt before this souvenir of his former military life with an offering of liquid metal cleaner and ceremoniously rubbed away any taint of the Western World. Fingerprints never marred the gleaming surface that reflected, to the relic-filled cage, the yellowed figure solicitously attending his inanimate idols.

Mr. Sears leaped and writhed in front of his door, awkwardly stabbing at my liquefied memories while spluttering.

'Shameful! I shall summon the police.'

Boysie swung a hob-nailed boot and kicked the large bronze gong standing just inside the door. The effect was astounding. The motorcyclists stopped practising for Brand's Hatch and lined up at the kerb. Mr. Sears' sword swung like a piece of forked lightning.

'Boysie, what is it?'

'Wanna talk to ya, don't I?'

'That's great, in the middle of the night. Send all your pals home or the law will play Happy Families with us all.'

'Dontcha want a ride on my mate's bike first? Oi, Don, give Miss MacMichael a ride.'

'Thanks awfully, Boysie, but I'm not really dressed for it.' My negligée swept from under the short racoon coat, bare bunions adhering to the pavement with icicle glue.

'Boysie, it's freezing. Send them home.'

'She don't want no ride. Push off you geezers. I'll see you at the Crown tomorrow night.'

The city's monarch dismissed his attendants with a wave of the knuckleduster. We shinnied up the bannisters, wriggling our hips in time to the music of twenty motorcycles taking off towards the Common.

Sears poked the sword through the rotten ceiling.

'I won't have it. I've never seen anything like this in my life.'

'New experiences are good for us all.'

Mr. Sears slammed his door downstairs and it reverberated through the flimsy house. I moulded the felt walls into a sitting-room and struggled with the paraffin heater for warmth. I fought with the light switch for light. Nothing in the house worked except Mr. Sears' mouth. Twenty-seven days later the heater burped forth greasy black smoke and one tiny flame. The fatty soot caked on to walls and the felt petrified into a five-foot thick stone coffin. One small bunion thawed over the flame while the bare bulb blinked off and on in Morse Code.

'All right, now, what is it?'

'I've just made a lot of money.'

Boysie usually made a lot of money and I sweated stale black smoke. One damaged nerve tapped out my rules in Morse in unison with the flashing light. 1: Never look or act shocked. 2: Discuss but do not lecture or moralize. Scathingly Seamus pronounced my guidelines pure crap. Through adherence to these precepts I had been rewarded by the trust and confidence of several students, and had also received giant skimmers of mould and dirt which, dumped into my left earhole, overflowed into my curly brain. A mind full of sewage, running races and holding swimming competitions, infecting and immunizing.

'How did you make the money?'

'Well, you know how they sell acid up the High Street?'

'Um-hum.'

'Well, see, I got some Coca-Cola and some sugar cubes and put a drop of Coke on each cube. I sold the cubes for a pound apiece. Dumb geezers thought I was pushing acid. Know something? Some of those gits took the stuff and got high. Just thinking it was the real stuff. High on sugar and Coke. Fucking hell.'

He flopped in the chair with laughter.

'So what happened to the money?'

'Oh yeah. I made four hundred quid on the stuff but what the hell can I do with that much money? If I took that home my old girl'd have a nag until she found out where it came from. I'd put it in the bank and have the Bill on my ass tomorrow. I can't buy gear with it cause the old girl'd want to know about the money for those, too. She'd just never stop having her nag. Nag, nag.'

'Well, what are you going to do with it?'

'I've already done it. I stood up the Common and handed it out to people what went by. By the fivers. I got rid of it all in an hour.'

'I notice you didn't think of your poverty-stricken teacher.'

He was genuinely horrified. Pounding feet banged on the floor and the black fuzz on his head wiggled back and forth.

'Jesus, Miss, you wouldn't take that kind of money, would you?'

Fleeting visions of paying my debts leered at me through the smoke.

'Of course not. Don't be so stupid.'

'Well I just thought I better tell you so if you hear anything you'll know I'm clean. Oh yeah, say, can you lend me eightpence for a ride on the night bus? Don buggered off and it's a fucking long walk home, ain't it?'

'Yes, sure. Look out for the man downstairs on your way out. He may try and catch you for a specimen to hang on his wall.'

'Bollocks to that. He won't catch nothing ever again if he tries that shit with me. Ta-ta, Miss.'

'Bye, Boysie.'

CHAPTER SEVEN

This was not the first conversation with Boysie, or any of my students, to take place outside school hours. Like many of his peers, Boysie found it impossible to express himself verbally unless he was physically occupied. As I lacked money but was blessed with a decrepit, mouldering flat, I was able to provide an endless variety of tasks for the boys. Once a week they arrived after school prepared to paint walls, sand furniture, cook, re-wire, think and talk.

Boysie's paralysing honesty revealed a deep curiosity regarding life. He was searching desperately to identify reasons for his own behaviour patterns. Given enough work, a nine-foot ear into which he could stumble, and a dearth of sermonizing, he began painfully to discover the motives for his actions.

The current, overwhelming problem was his family's emigration to New Zealand. His parents fantasied the foreign country as a modern land of milk, honey, manna and money. Good wages, social acceptance, a lovely home and motor car awaited their descent from the elegant steamship. Boysie perceived the move in stark realism, and he was terrified at the prospect. They would move from a self-created slum dwelling in England to one in New Zealand. Shredded wallpaper, steps rotten and decaying, ripped and unwashed curtains, and the interminable reek of rancid oil were the more favourable aspects of the present home. None of the beds had sheets, heaps of dirty laundry decorated the cracked and frayed lino. An old, partially-dismantled lorry had rusted for four years in the weeds behind the council house. Sun might beat down in New Zealand but home would be the same.

Boysie had discovered that a family is barred from New Zealand if one of the members has a criminal record and he was trying to get inside. The obstacle was his intelligence and native cunning. He could never allow himself to be caught.

He ran with a gang. Sometimes two or three gangs, I gathered. Whenever there was a rumble he and his mates met the opposing side, or sides as the case might be, using knives, chains and bottles. Invariably the law and the ambulances broke into the fray.

'Why haven't you ever been caught or hurt, Boysie?' We sanded down a splintered bookcase. Boysie used sandpaper. I used my jagged fingernails.

'I use me loaf, don't I? Me fucking mates always go to a punch-up in jeans, boots and leather jackets. Stupid gits. Me, I put on me best suit and shirt. Even a tie, and I hate fucking ties. Can't breathe.'

He emitted a strangled cough and turned lavender in demonstration. I scraped on with my nails.

'Oi, like these shoes? They're new aren't they?'

'They're lovely. I do like lemon suede. And?'

'Oh yeah. When the Bill comes I just walk back into the bushes, climb over a fence to the next street and walk back into the cops. In me gear I've never even been stopped. Cops don't look at anyone wearing a suit coming right at them. Never walk the otherway, though. Gotta use your wick, dont-cha?

'Never been hurt because I know most of the geezers on both sides. Like last week I was in this punch-up at the Crown, see, and I had me razor. I guess I stabbed two or three gits, but no one got me. Every time they'd just look and say, "Oh, it's you, Boysie". I never get hurt. Little cut here and there but not hurt.'

'Did the ones you stabbed live?'

'Huh? Oh. Dunno. Don't know who they were, do I?'

'Then why stab them?'

'Kicks.'

'I don't think that's kicks. Do you really?'

'Oh, guess it's not. Guess I musta been pilled. Dunno, I guess. Hey, I stomped on this one geezer and got this off his neck. Want it?'

He took something out of a very scruffy wallet. I blew the sawdust out of my cracked nails and looked at his hand. A silver crucifix lay dying on the dirty calluses.

'Go on, take it. It don't mean nothing to me.'

'No thanks, Boysie. You should try and give it back to the man.'

'Naw, fuck that. Don't know who he was, do I? Sure you don't want it? Then I'll keep it. Might bring me luck.'

My gut flapped its filigree antennae and noshed on a maggot as Christ slapped up and down against his chest.

I wrapped around the paraffin heater, avidly absorbing soot and dirt. Shaking the day's rancid litter from my clogged brain, I dried it over the smoking heater and carefully rearranged the disordered folds. I applied iodine to three festering nerve ends and encased one lacerated emotion in dirty plaster. Cold crackled from the five-foot thick, peeling walls and showered down on the smouldering heater in translucent slivers that slid to the floor and heaped over my bunions. I blew black mucus from my nose into an iced handkerchief that cracked and mutilated my upper lip. Leaning over the heater I bathed in raw paraffin fumes that spiralled towards the blackened ceiling in frosty circles. Through the gloom of smoke, cold and solid fuel I saw the door open, and Boysie entered.

'Boysie, how in the hell did you get in?'

'Picked the lock downstairs, didn't I? Gotta keep in practice. You 'otta get that changed, Miss. Anybody'd get in here. Hey, I'm going up to the Crown to a dance. You like this suit?'

He was wearing a double-breasted, brown flannel suit with flaring bell-bottom trousers. Under the long jacket he was shirtless and vestless, his chest covered with a hideous tattoo.

'I think it's lovely, Boysie. Very chic indeed.'

'The old girl's wild to know how I can pay for it.'

'So how can you pay for it?'

'Last weekend two of me mates and I nicked a lorry, see, and went to the Park. You know all those sheep in the Park? We nicked all that we could stuff into the lorry and then drove up north and sold them on the market. I got about thirty quid meself for the fucking things. You really like this suit? I've gotta get a girl at the dance tonight.'

'You'll have all the girls after you in that suit. You aren't going without a shirt, though, are you?'

'Why not? I get hot when I go dancing.'

'Because that tattoo on your chest doesn't look very well with the suit. A shirt really would be better. Unless you know girls who like to dance with two lion's eyes watching them from under a jacket. What happened to the lorry?'

'Drove it over the tip, didn't we? Bill won't find it there for months, if they ever do. Say, what do you want for Christmas?'

'For you to stay out of the nick.'

'I mean really.'

'I mean really, too.'

'Oh yeah, sure. I'll try. That's no fucking Christmas present, though. If I don't get nicked I'm going to find meself on that boat.'

'Boysie, you're going to find yourself on it, so think

about the sun in New Zealand. While we freeze to death here you will be splashing around on some sweltering beach, turning tan and – (oh Lord!) – at least looking healthy.'

It was the best effort I could manage at the moment. Actually the thought appealed tremendously to me, as I blew more grey soot from my nostrils and held frozen lashes up with my chilblains.

'Bugger the sun. Who wants to fucking look black? I'm going out and get pilled. You really think I should put on a shirt? Bugger! All right, then, a shirt.'

Boysie liked my cooking, particularly because it was hot and spicy.

'These fucking English don't know how to eat They ain't got no taste, Miss. Now I'm going to cook you somethin' we used to have in the Cape. Me old girl showed me how.'

He arrived with pots, pans and ingredients strapped on to his motorcycle, brought them upstairs in three trips, and began to brew up cuisine of the Cape.

'You read in the papers about that office building? The one where they're still looking for the people what done it?'

'Um hum, I read it. Why?'

A few days before a building and adjoining factory had been smashed, burned and looted. The premises had been completely demolished and the damage was estimated to be in the millions. The person or persons responsible for the vandalism had escaped without leaving trace or clue. So said the newspapers, anyway.

'Me and Don done that.'

He hacked away at several enormous onions.

'Stone me! These buggers make me eyes cry.'

'Does Seamus know about it?'

'Yeah. Don't know how he found out. Nobody else knows except me 'nd Don. And now you.'

Somebody else must know.

'What did he say?'

'Made me tell him why I done it. Fuck these buggers!' He threw the onions into a pot and began whacking away at a chunk of mutton.

'You wanna know why? It was New Zealand. S'truth, wish I hadn't 'uv run when the Bill got there.'

He whittled at some garlic while I scrubbed at my mind with Ajax and sprinkled baby powder in the creases.

'You're going to like this, Miss. Gotta have rice with it, though. Got any rice around this dump?'

Boysie squatted on the bedroom floor ineptly splashing black paint on the wooden base board. His offer to help me paint the flat was conditional: he must be allowed to choose the colours for the bedroom.

'Always wanted to decorate me own room but the old girl never let me.'

I had reluctantly allowed Boysie to choose my bedroom colour scheme and now found my sleeping quarters vibrating with one tangerine and three scarlet walls, a fuchsia ceiling and black woodwork. I groaned. Silently he slapped black gloss on the peeling wood, liberally dousing my newly sanded floor with glistening black drops.

'Boysie, put newspapers on the floor, please. You can't get that paint off without sanding it again.'

'Yeah, Miss.' He continued to splatter the area with black gloss. I tried again.

'Boysie, the papers are right behind you. You'll save yourself a lot of work later if you use them now.'

'Yeah.' He leaned back and squinted critically at the wall and woodwork. 'Think it's O.K., Miss?'

'Beautiful.'

He began to work again with renewed vigour. 'Oi, ya know who I saw today? Jenny. In the High Street with some geezer in orange strides. *Orange!* Stone me! Haven't seen her for a month maybe.'

He dropped the brush into the paint pot and absently sloshed the bristles up and down.

'Jeeeesus! I used ta think I was in love with her. Ya ever been in love, Miss?'

'Not really.'

His black fuzz wrinkled and the brown eyes rounded in disbelief. Forgotten, the paint brush sank into a foot of black gloss as Boysie wrapped both arms around his bent legs.

'S'truth! Never? How d'ya know if you are?'

'When I am I'll tell you the answer to that one.'

Leaning back against the wall he examined one black-rimmed window.

'I used ta give Jenny presents. Ya know, stuff like shoes and dresses and coats. Real smart gear. She never wanted ta go nowhere, though. Just to bed. If me and me mates went to a dance we went without her. Pictures, too. All she wanted was just a poke.'

Chin resting on one knee, he prodded at a fissure in the floor.

'One time her old girl come in and found us having it off in her front room.'

'What happened?'

'She didn't know what was going on, did she?'

'Oh come on, Boysie, nobody's mother is that stupid.'

'Jenny was sitting on me, wasn't she? On a chair. I pulled her dress down and the old girl just stood there moaning away about her Bingo night. Jesus! Then she asked if we want a cup of tea. How're we going to get up for a cuppa bloody char? Finally she goes out and gets it for us. Never did know. Another time we was in our front room and my Dad walks in. There's Jenny and me banging away on the sofa and all he says is 'be careful'. Fucking hell! I been in Jenny's knickers for a year and all he can say is be careful. It's daft.'

Boysie shook his head, perplexed at adult logic. He didn't look at me.

'Whatd'ya reckon, Miss? Jenny don't know how to talk and she don't want to go nowhere with me. If all she wants is presents and a cock all the time is that love?'

'No, I shouldn't think it is.'

'Yeah, that's what I thought.'

He reached into the paint pot and fished for the brush.

'Sod this. Lookit the handle. Oi, gimme them papers, Miss.'

Two days later Boysie was nicked for stealing two bottles of beer. Seamus went to court with him, as he did with all the students, and Boysie was released with a warning. Not even probation. He was going to New Zealand.

CHAPTER EIGHT

It was almost Christmas and the children had stayed out of trouble, or at least out of any serious difficulty. That would all change over the holiday as it always did. Free time, for these children, was an enigma: another curse bestowed upon the rejects by a condemning society. They were completely unable to fill the unwanted leisure hours with an acceptable activity. They could not read, did not work, lacked money for bowling or swimming, and were quickly bored by a surfeit of television at home. So they drifted into exciting, cost-free pursuits. Arson, soliciting, shoplifting and larceny were the favoured adventures during any holiday.

Our students were fairly wild before the holidays began, too. 'Separation complex,' Seamus pronounced with an authoritative wave of his parchment fingers. They were also wild when the wind blew, when the rain kept them inside, when it was time for the full moon, when it snowed, and when it was cloudy and moist. I think it fair to say that I had never seen the children when they were not wild.

Three tables, pushed together, almost filled the staff room. We jammed inside, squeezing between the wall and tables, legs laced, elbows tied with tinsel, and prepared for 'Christmas Dinner'. This was the humorous title given by the cook to lunch on the last day before holiday. Our chef was totally devoid of talent in the culinary arts, but on this festive day the quantity of food she offered was compensation for any lack of skill in its preparation.

I unlocked my neck and looked around at the assembled staff. 'Social occasion' faces were sealed to transparent, rubber heads. Seamus passed out paper hats. God, how I hated paper hats. Noodle arms raised in unison and placed them on the balloons. I used mine as a serviette.

I locked my neck again and my eyes wandered around the room's equator. Numerous balloons with appropriate, identical expressions, a truant officer, someone's husband, and an old lady who apparently mistook this for the Co-op. Lady, this ain't no Co-op but eat up anyway.

'I want dry, Seamus. I really can't bear sweet.'

'Come on, let's sing.'

Oh God, that was just all we needed. Two things I hated most were paper hats and community songs.

'Conor, your glass is empty.'

'It's always empty because I drink fast.'

A grim smile from Sir as he passed me a bottle of something marked 'demi-sec'. I poured out a glass and drank it down. Great good merciful God. Made in Britain from home-grown grapes, tramped down with home-grown, unwashed feet and bottled in a speeding lorry. Never mind, we weren't at Claridges.

Una was always drunk on one glass of wine. She had consumed two and was seated on my left alternately singing dirty songs composed spontaneously and belching loudly.

I stabbed at a dry pellet that closely resembled a goat turd. British demi-sec congealed in my stomach as I thought of Barbara tethered in the animal pen. I speculated on the cook's sense of humour and her methods of stretching a meagre Christmas dinner.

'Just for safety's sake, what are these little balls?'

Mabel turned towards me, dragging a strand of greasy hair through the mashed potato. She flicked it back and the white blob soared up. Someone's social face remained in place as a bloated hand delicately fished out the granite chip and tossed it into the plate. Clunk.

'Bacon rolls, dear. An English speciality.'

'I can't get it on to my fork, so pardon the fingers. Pretend I'm Gaylord for a minute.'

I bit on the 'English speciality' and a tooth cracked. I sighed and probed the fissure with my furry tongue. I had been in England three years and had never broken a tooth on the food before. This was, however, the first time I had been served a 'speciality'.

I spat the goat-dropping into my paper hat.

'I'm going to bill the Department of Education for a new tooth next week.'

Strained laughter. Mabel said:

'Well, they are a bit better when I make them at home.'

I shall light a candle for homes all over England making bacon rolls this Christmastide.

'Forget this bloody special food and concentrate on the wine, while there's still some left.'

Identical thoughts converged on the alcohol, and they proceeded to empty the bottles in a refined, surreptitious manner. I drank off another glass of wine. They began on the carols and I considered drinking straight from the bottle. What a farce. With the exception of Una and myself, every member of staff loathed and feared every other one. They either did not know, or had forgotten, that an entire world existed outside these school gates. Life, for each of them, consisted of school and home, the two connected by a shiny mirrored umbilical tube, and an assortment of faces from which to choose. Petty jealousies, power struggles, frustrated ambitions and hatreds emerged in the Staff Room. The Staff feared Boysie but envied his ability to achieve what they themselves could not: he could stab someone and get away with it. I gulped another glass of homegrown wine and looked at Mabel who suddenly had two identical heads. I didn't care what they said or thought of me. I was an unqualified teacher anyway. I hiccuped an evil mixture of acid wine and bitter laughter and drank from the bottle, dribbling wine over my serviette. Seamus glared. I prayed that they would stop singing *God Rest Ye Merry Gentlemen* and limped back into my mind. Unqualified. Four years' training and a degree recognized by the University of London. Three years of teaching in the States. One year of social work. Testimonials. Recommendations. Allow me to unfurl my life so that you can blow your nose on it. It was American, not English or Commonwealth, and the Department of Education is not required to recognize American degrees. There are no rules and no lists.

'My dear, if you had graduated from Yale it would be acceptable, I can assure you of that.'

You must be a nutter. Yale is a men's university. Do I look like a man?

'Well it is too bad you aren't a man. With a Yale degree, of course.'

It's too bad I'm teaching in England you mean. Must be the magnificent salary that attracts me.

I wiggled my toes through the hole in my right shoe and thought of all the locked doors labelled 'Qualification' upon which I had hammered. Grinning Union Jacks had crawled from underneath the floorboards. Apparently I was sufficiently competent, as a teacher, to be hired, but not good enough to be paid for my efforts. *My* shoes were the ones with holes, and it was *my* stomach that rumbled, but as long as I taught well no one listened.

I emptied the bottle and studied the chattering balloons.

What a school. A real mind-splitter. No teacher ever stayed here for very long. Slow strangulation by the toxic pus-pot would occur, usually complicated by a nasty fall from the fragile stage. Eventually a stiletto heel or a sharpened eyeball gouged a hole in the mirrored casing between home and school and the stifling teacher gasped in the fresh, clean air of an outside world. They mended damaged emotions, repaired lacerated nerves, carefully folded the masks in tissue paper and left.

'Seamus, some more of that rot-gut, please.'

He looked pained.

'That rot-gut is my Christmas gift to the Staff.'

'Thanks very much. Could I have some of the gift in that bottle? The green one. Maybe it's magic leprechaun wine and I'll find the treasure.'

They began to carve up *Away in a manger* just as hammering was heard on the door, accompanied by unintelligible screams. Seamus' chair was wedged against the door, and he glided from the seat and rippled to the table top in jellied segments. Several rubber arms leaped to his aid.

'Help him up on the table.'

'Come on, help him up.'

'. . . get that arm.'

'Stand on that side, that's it. Jolly good.'

Chair in one hand, glass of wine delicately poised in the other, Seamus postured on the table as the door bounced open. Several children skittered about in fright and excitement.

'Come quick! Quick! Leroy's gone spare.'

'He's gonna kill Abel.'

'He found those wine bottles in Miss MacMichael's room and he's slinging them all over . . .'

Seamus was lowered gracefully to the floor and slithered rapidly down the corridor, with the staff in pursuit. The students had been unsupervised during our celebrations, which was a violation of school rules. Drinking in school during school hours was certainly not encouraged by the Department either. The staff ran faster, swept along by the Chief Education Officer's wrathful ghost.

Passing the front door I looked through the glass towards my classroom. A bottle hit one of my windows and the pane bulged, contracted, and shattered as the bottle erupted through it and hit the pavement. I belted down the corridor.

Bunches of cellophane children choked the doorway to my classroom. Printed eyes stared into the room as they crouched, ready to run, on wrapping-paper Chelsea boots that pointed down the hallway. I tore my way through the mass of paper, my head jumping up and down on a rubber band. Damn everybody! We lacked art supplies of any kind, and I had been collecting bottles to use in creating glass and cement mosaic blocks. Knowing that they were potential weapons but lacking storage space I had been keeping the bottles underneath the sink. Unfortunately, Leroy had an entire arsenal to hand when he lost control, attributable to my feeble attempt to provide craft for the students. I was a 'loser'.

I pushed into the silent room and stopped. Seamus stood on centre stage, confronting Leroy, Boysie and Victor. He brushed at invisible dust on his pin stripe suit, and the veined hand shook with rage. Reptilian eyes crackled grey flames and illuminated the decayed face. His hoarse voice quivered in anger.

'Well? What the hell is it now? Interrupting my Christmas dinner. I'm talking to you, blubber lips!'

Leroy, a new student from West Africa, was defiant.

'He called me a black bastard. Nobody calls me that. I'll cut his fucking balls off, Sir!'

'Who did?' Seamus stopped flicking at the suit and his eyes snaked over to Victor. He slowly polished one gold ring on the jacket.

'Abel. No one calls me that. No o . . .'

'For Christ's sake *belt up*. Where's Abel?'

Boysie slouched against the blackboard, pulling at one ear-lobe.

'He ran into the bog-hole when Leroy threw a bottle at him.'

'I'll have that coon sent down! Mabel, see that a note goes to his father tonight, and I want a written answer in the morning.' Mabel beamed. 'Tell him that I won't have a fifteen-year-old delinquent rocking my school. I'm running this place, and anyone that gets in my way goes out. Abel starts trouble and then hides in the urinal. You know what the rest of you are? *Mugs!* You're stupid, bloody mugs!'

Seamus tap-danced around the stage, and slid to a stop. Pulling a linen handkerchief from his breast pocket he examined it minutely for flaws and specks of dirt. Satisfied, he removed the gold ring, and polished it on the handkerchief.

'For God's sake, someone go and get Abel! Great, stupid oafs.'

Paper shoes crunched down the corridor as the students ran for Abel. Unpopular with his peers, he was dragged from the loo and shoved into the classroom where he stood, stabbing at the floor with an enormous motorcycle boot.

Seamus replaced the ring on his finger and held his parchment hand to the light, carefully scrutinizing the ornament. He frowned and transferred the gold object to a finger on the other hand. Snapping imaginary soil from the linen square, he arranged it in his breast pocket and glowered at Abel.

'Damn it! Don't you have any common at all? Don't you know the rules after four years here?'

'Sir.'

'What's this about picking on Leroy? I hate a bully, and that's about all you're good for. Bully a twelve-year-old boy. I wish to God one of those bottles had hit your thick head.'

'He threw a bottle at me.'

'Well *why*?'

'I called him a name, Sir.'

'What name?'

Abel's head hung towards the floor and he watched the huge boot scuffing at the wooden floor. One hand was crammed into a tattered jacket pocket, and the other absently scratched at his scabrous scalp.

'*Answer me!* What name?'

'Black bastard.'

'You stupid great coon. You haven't learned one damned thing at this school. I wish I'd sent you down that last time in court. I'm sending a letter to your father tonight and you know what that means? Uh? You'll get that belt buckle on your stupid arse so hard that you won't sit down for a week. Great bully. Start trouble and then run like hell. And look at your *feet*. For Christ's sake, *take those damned boots off*! The rules are to wear plimsolls in school, and you damned well know it. You want to ruin this floor?' Everyone stared at the ancient, battered floor, worn and marred beyond repair.

'You, Leroy. You haven't been here long, just about five minutes, but we don't behave like this here. You want to throw bottles, you throw them at me and see what happens. Want to have a go? Uh?'

Leroy stared unhappily at the gaunt, wrathful figure that flashed hatred and ire from grey, opaque eyes.

'No, Sir.'

Seamus adjusted his tie, stretching the withered cords of his neck as the silk noose tightened.

'I'll tell you what you and Abel are going to do now. You're going to measure that window and go home for some money. Then you'll buy a new pane of glass and put it in. Mr. Jackson will help you with it if you don't know how. Then you two are going to sweep up the front walk and clean up this room. I never want this repeated. Clear?'

'Yes, Sir.'

'Yes, Sir.'

'And what were you and Victor doing? *Boysie!* I'm talking to you.'

Victor was vomiting out of the window on to the splintered glass. The students watched in fascination.

'We was trying ta stop Leroy before he fucked up the whole bloody room, Sir. He went spare.'

'I know that. You have anything else to do with the trouble?'

'No, Sir.'

'All right, good lads. Abel and Leroy, get going. The rest of you, into the hall. You're going to sit and have a fifteen-minute think before we begin classes.'

They tumbled down the corridor into the hall. Victor was still vomiting. Seamus descended from the stage and, tracing one ochre wrinkle under his lidless eye, snaked down the hallway. Merry Christmas and God do please rest ye Merry Gentlemen.

CHAPTER NINE

CHUNKS of sea salt furrowed my coral rouge. They plummeted to the floor and burst into flame amidst tiny slivers of heart. My soul slid into the trashbin and pulled up the covers.

'Why does he have to go to New Zealand? It's a rotten waste. Just waste! You know what will happen to him there? It will all be lost, all the time, all the effort, everything. Damn it, Seamus, *do* something.'

Hard chips of solidified mineral striated my face. Blood, rouge, green mucus and gangrenous emotions dripped on to his desk.

'Oh don't cry. For God's sake, *stop it*. Can't do anything. I've talked to his mother and the parents want to go. I've told her that it's the worst thing for all the children but she doesn't want to know. I'm not very happy about it myself, you know.'

Seamus undulated away from the desk, a white hanky draped over one scaly index finger. He stood up and shrank to the floor, proffering the linen cloth. I took it and he adjusted his silk tie.

I bent down to look. He had sent boys to Borstal, conned the kind-hearted out of pounds and possessions and boasted, leaning on his cane carved from solid fear, that he could do anything. 'This is *my* school and I run it. Alone. It belongs to me. Mine.' Three quarters of one inch high.

'We have to admit that this is one of our failures. We can't do a thing about it.' (Now it was 'we'.) 'The family is going to New Zealand and we just write Boysie off as a loss. It's too bad.'

A marble tear dropped on to his wavy white hair. He pulled out a slim, mother-of-pearl comb.

Too bad. Too bad. Boysie was one of the few students at St. Steven's with real potential, and he was probably the only one who would, eventually, be a success. As a vocation he might choose farming, crime or union politics, but the selected career would be exceptional. And he would do it well. Tiny phantoms appeared behind the floodlights on Seamus' desk. Reformed delinquent in middle age. Non-readers who could now read *The Racing World*. They were all bank messengers. No nicking. They methodically and reliably delivered important papers and went to the local at six o'clock after tea. They were arranged in a circle on the desk top, and in the centre were twin Boysies. One was strapped into an electric chair; the other seated in a Ferrari. Yes, he would be damned good at something.

I shouted over the eight miles to Seamus.

'Just six months more, Seamus. That's all I want. He can read now, by then he will be able to read himself, his motives. You could keep him. Be his guardian. Just for six months.'

'Can't hear you.' He combed his hair.

'I know a man in immigration. You could ring him and have the visas cancelled.'

'Sacrifice the family for him? I couldn't do that. There are twelve others in that family you know. I wouldn't play God.'

Seamus had never before hesitated to emulate the deity, but this role, like any of his characterizations, was played only at his own instigation. He wrote, directed and produced. It was *his* school.

Seamus jumped on the see-saw and towered over me.

'You have to be tough in this game. Hard. You aren't hard enough. Go on home and get hard.'

I wrapped myself around a tear and rolled out under the door. Behind me Seamus combed his hair and read my salted crystals.

'What the hell's she on about? Think of others. Gaylord and Stewart. Marrie. Bugger.'

CHAPTER TEN

I SLIPPED on a glacier in the pavement.

Damn.

Next time I would try my ice skates.

Winter in England was lovely if you lived in a warm flat, owned some fur-lined boots, and had enough to eat. I didn't like England in winter.

I pushed open the middle-class gate and fell over one

thousand eggshells. Jesus, what a pong. Just like the kids in assembly. Wonder if they've decided to spend the holiday prone on my front lawn. I crawled over the eggshells and strained to see through the air, black and segmented with cold. Great God. All the dustbins in the street had been dragged inside the hedge and tipped over the lawn. Mildewed potatoes nestled on beds of decayed bones, tin cans with festering remnants of baked beans peeped from beneath well-saturated wrappers, heaps of ancient tea-leaves crowned green bread crusts, and a broken whisky bottle adorned a collection of rust-tinged lettuce leaves. Unfortunately, the odour from this brown bottle was the only smell obliterated in the sewage that was strewn in grand, quivering array before my front door. I slid to the door on a bacon rind, stopping my nostrils with one hand and fished for the key with the other.

Inside, I dumped my bag and books to the floor and they immediately disappeared under a grainy mass. I tried to lift one foot and found that both legs had sunk to the kneecaps. Sand. Sand covering the floor of my front hall on the coldest night London had endured for three years. I slapped at the wall for the light switch and missed. Uncovering my right foot, I picked it up and squinted at the gritty matter. The bacon rind, still clinging to my left shoe, skidded and I thumped on to my arse, burrowing into the sticky meal. It packed into my hair, scratched under my contact lenses, festooned my false eyelashes and ground into my teeth. I licked a bit from my lower lip, then licked some more. God, it was sugar! I sat up and crawled to the wall, showering sugar from my coated arms as I scraped and poked about the doorway for the light switch. Glorious light from a bare, forty-watt bulb illuminated the hall. Eight pounds of sugar had been pushed through the mail slot. Empty bags peered at me from the top of the heap and laughed.

The students thought that I had moved, and this was a Christmas gift to the city's most popular accountant.

Happy last day of school to me. I rode upstairs on the bacon rind and washed my hair.

A feeble fist, weary from long days spent attending to money, pounded on my door. Buttoning up my dignity and sticking on my eyelashes I confronted Mr. Sears.

His arms flapped and he executed an intricate toe-dance on the step. Eyeballs expanded and contracted with each heartbeat, and his head jerked back and forth.

'Yes?'

'You. You. Why? What's the meaning ...' For once speech failed him, and his voice floated down to hide under a pile of rotten tea leaves covering the path.

I suddenly realized that he thought I was responsible for the chaos that shimmered and smelt downstairs.

'Mr. Sears, I think you need psychiatric help. If I could afford that much sugar I would have made you some lovely American Christmas cookies. Specialities. For your teeth. And now, if you'll excuse me, I'm going to bed. Merry Christmas!'

I took off my dignity, pressed out all the wrinkles, and shivered my way into bed. Downstairs the Hoover gargled granulated sugar. I rolled over and puffed up the pillow with laughter. Ho-ho for Anglo-American relations.

CHAPTER ELEVEN

Christmas was over. Boysie's family had sailed for New Zealand on an enormous liner that radiated unmitigated luxury. It boasted several bars, a tiny swimming-pool, and stopped in South Africa. Bit daft for a Cape-coloured family to waltz around Cape Town with the rest of the passengers I thought. Boysie didn't sail with them. He wove a Purple Heart cocoon, climbed in and flew to New Zealand.

We returned to school for the winter term.

'Staff meeting. Staff meeting right now.'

I kicked Una and purred.

'Wait for the Winter Surprise in Our Very Own Staff Room.'

'What I'm waiting for is autumn when I can get out of this madhouse.'

She was leaving for good in the autumn. For a year she had threatened to leave and had given notice twice. Each time Seamus had carefully unwrapped his best Irish charm and hooked it over an imitation-gold tooth.

'I can't let you go, Una. What will I do without you? You're the only one really loyal to me. No one works as hard as you, or is as patient. I'll give you more free time. An easier class. Just reconsider. Don't leave. We need you. I need you.'

Una left the office and charm was solicitously placed in the sarcophagus. Seamus adjusted his fang dentures and spat venom at the closed door. It drooled down the wooden panels and spread over the floor in an undulating quicksand mire.

'Neurotic bitch! She causes all the trouble in this school. Bringing her home troubles in here and upsetting the kids. I've known more wogs than any of you and I can tell you she's typical. Flirts with any man around, but I'll bet she's frigid. I wish she'd drop dead . . .'

He brought new linen handkerchiefs for Una to embroider. I puked, and she withdrew her notice again.

We crammed into the staff room. Plastic orbs wore noncommittal expressions as Seamus examined a gold signet ring. Wrinkles greyed and the rope cheeks contracted as he adjusted himself behind the desk. Silently he passed out the mimeographed sheets.

Change was essential to the rotting structure of this plaster theatre. It reinforced fear and generated a choking vapour of instability that suffocated the children as they groped desperately for some solid object to which to cling. Scenery dissolved into dust stew as the frantic students clawed for a hand-hold to life. Emotionally deprived and unable to adjust because their lives were based in rejection and rootless instability, we provided final assurance that they were worthless refuse, necessary as props on a decaying stage.

If an academic programme proved successful and satisfactory, it was altered. Daily activities were unscheduled and subject to Seamus' shifting moods and impulses. There was no timetable for the bells and classes were, as a result, disorganized and unsettled. Breaks and lunchtimes were haphazard. Seamus encouraged outdoor labour as part of the 'therapy' and often lessons were completely abandoned for weeks so that we could dig trenches. Once dug, Seamus directed that they be filled in again and redug. Weeks were spent chopping brambles and undergrowth in the woods. Staff and children suffered from infected hands, sore muscles and exhausted tempers. Roots were untreated and the area disused and our performance was repeated six months later. Huge trees were felled in random fashion, the logs sawn and a wall was partially constructed. Before completion the project was abandoned for no apparent reason. Sheds constructed, razed and re-built two feet from the original site. Classes were shuffled every term, no student remaining with the same teacher or classmates for more than three months. If a student was particularly suited to one class and progressed in this atmosphere, he was the first to be transferred to another class.

Change was the corrosive sellotape at St. Steven's, and we were gathered to receive word of the latest alterations.

'Over the holidays I've been thinking that we need a new arrangement of classes. Fresh teachers for the students. New approaches to their problems. We can't allow ourselves to become stultified in this type of school. Now if you will look at your papers you'll find the new lists of students for each teacher.'

I looked. Roberts, Cheney, O'Rafferty, Jamison, King, Gregory, Silver. *Silver. Gaylord.* You rotten dirty son-of-a-bitch.

Blood drained out through my toe nails. I looked around the room. They were rapidly applying smirks.

'I won't have Gaylord. I won't have these others either. They're all the ones who test out sub-normal. They're stupid. I'm no good with stupid kids. I don't like them.'

'We can't afford to dislike *any* child here.' Rancid oil and sugared tea. They quickly substituted expressions of approval and bent towards Seamus.

'All right. I don't dislike them, but I don't want them either.'

'You are good with the tearaways. Very good indeed. See what you can do with these. Spend lots of time on reading.'

'With *Gaylord* in the class? I want the tearaways.'

'Well you don't have them. Or can't you cope? A good teacher can cope with anything.'

Well I'm a lousy teacher and my head aches and I want a mask too. 'I won't take Gaylord.'

Una skirted round the quicksand towards the door.

'Conor can do it, of course. I'll help her with Gaylord at any time. But you can get stuffed, Seamus. All of you.'

Button up the dignity and adjust your eyelashes. Knees up, stomach in, back straight. March, two, three.

Outside I sagged on to the fishtank.

'Una, I *can't*. I can't do it. I'm terrified when Gaylord's in the same room. That sadistic bastard has put Tina in my class too, and Gaylord's always trying to kill her. I can't. I'm sick.'

'Yes you can. You aren't going to let that egotistical fool beat you. He's just trying to break you down the way he broke me. You've never said can't in your life, so don't start now. You've come through hell thumbs up, so do it now. Come on, we'll fight him.'

O.K. Fight. Lead the little children into battle. Choose sides, gang. We went into assembly and sang *Onward Christian Soldiers.*

Seamus read out the list of new classes. Marrie jumped up. 'Fuck that. I want back in Miss MacMichael's class. Miss, he gave you the dumb ones. I want in your class. I won't do any work for that pissy teacher I have now. I want Miss MacMichael.'

'That's enough!'

'Sir.'

The students had been shuffled and dealt. I sat on my desk and scratched the ceiling. God. What could I *do*? Tina was the only student in school with a reading age exceeeding her chronological age. She was a mouse with an IQ. Jeff was a complete non-reader. Tony a slow reader. Basil dwelt in a world of monsters and homosexuality. Some world. Wouldn't be so bad if he were able to write about it. Margaret was a hypochondriac, suffering from an infected scar on the rectum which no specialist could detect. She couldn't read either. And Gaylord.

'Get out your pencils.'

They got them out. No one swore. No one spoke.

'Put away your pencils.'

They put them away.

'Go get your PT kits.'

They got the kits.

'Put them away.'

They did.

Pieces of soggy angel cake.

And Gaylord. He sat on the floor behind the piano and refused to move. Brown hands covered his face. I wished he would stay there for the term. Two stiff fingers separated into a slot through which he stared at me. Empty brown sockets that bulged with translucent Nothing. He giggled. I picked up the giggle and dropped it in the bin. He giggled again.

I'd rather have angel cake, please.

The second day of term Gaylord got up off the floor.

He had a catapult. Rubber bands for this toy were hidden in his socks, under his belt, in the crutch of his pants. He had an endless supply of craftily concealed bands. Seamus suggested that I strip him and search.

'For God's sake, don't run to me about it. You can handle Gaylord. He's just a sixteen-year-old boy. Take the damned bands away from him.'

So I let Gaylord keep the bands. He demanded constant attention from me, and reciprocated by pulling out the catapult and bands on whim. Nails, drawing pins and broken compass points, propelled by the hands, sprayed the blackboard behind me.

'I'm going to squash your eye.' Giggle.

He found scissors and threw them at my stomach.

'You leave me alone, you bitch.' Giggle.

He took a razor blade from Una's sewing kit, embedded it in wood and lunged over the desk at me.

'I'm going to cut off your tits.' Giggle.

Anything lethal was locked in my top desk drawer. Gaylord went through my bag and found the keys. I transferred all dangerous items to my bag and locked it in the staff room. Gaylord broke down the door and found the bag. During an outdoor work period he found a branch in the wood, sharpened it into a spear, and threw the stick at Tina's legs. He took a hammer from the caretaker's hut and sent it hurtling towards my head. He produced a saw and tried to amputate my left hand. The days were a kaleidoscope of Gaylord.

'Seamus, he's dangerous. He's going to kill someone sooner or later.'

'Bloody nonsense! You're just a rotten teacher. Gaylord's improving every day and you know it. When he came here he couldn't even speak. Get back to class and don't bother me about Gaylord again.'

Desperately I sought a way to control Gaylord and found that none of the standard methods apply to a psychotic boy. Teaching was forgotten in the interminable attempt to restrain Gaylord's fits of violence. Although I was unable to conquer my terror, I found that the deranged boy was alarmed by loud noises, and could be checked if I exhibited total fearlessness. I began keeping a large tin box of chalk bits on the desk. When Gaylord threw a knife, I shouted,

'Stop that at ONCE,' and threw the box to the floor. The noise, and my lack of fear, shocked Gaylord to a momentary standstill. A nail vaulted towards my eye and I broke a ruler on the desk top checking him once again. He ripped Tina's work book and I shattered a chair against the wall. School hours telescoped into incessant noise and pseudo-bravery pitted against the uncontrollable violence of a mad boy.

I'm just like Seamus. Wave my fear, make noises, show my courage. I don't want to be like this. I don't want Gaylord. I can't cope. I can't teach.

My students got out pencils, put them away, got out PT kits and put them away on signal while I threw chairs. They learned nothing, for I had no time to teach. Gaylord sawed at my mind and I hurled the chalk box through the window.

Gaylord refused to join the class in PT, hiding behind the piano while the others bent, stretched and ran on the spot. Seamus undulated into the room and stood, rubbing one pearl cuff-link.

'Where's Gaylord?'

'He won't put on his track suit, Seamus.'

'The hell he won't. *Gaylord!* Gaylord, man, get out here. You want a smack on the head? No? If you don't get into that track suit *now*, I'll flatten you.'

He cracked Gaylord on one ear and the boy turned stiffly to put on the track suit.

'I won't have this crap, Conor. The entire class is to

have one hour PT each day, and that includes Gaylord. You make him do it. It's your responsibility.'

The following day Gaylord refused to join in the exercises and I withheld his food. He stabbed me in the arm with a compass and I sent a desk drawer through the window. After three days he put on his track suit and tried to knife Tina in the chest. I hit him on the head. I had never struck a student before.

Two weeks later I was sick.

CHAPTER TWELVE

I HAD been coughing for more than two months. Prescribing my own cure, I smoked more cigarettes and sat up all night coughing and smoking while my stomach wept and my lungs dissolved. Finally, I paid a visit to the local doctor who diagnosed bronchitis and lung infection, presented me with an evil-looking magic potion, and sent me home to bed.

It was, I suppose, the result of inadequate clothing, improper food and appalling living conditions. My new flat was to me enormously attractive because it was cheap, isolated, and rat-free. It also lacked heat and hot water. Sashes on most of the windows were broken and snow and rain swept in, freezing on the walls and windowpanes. Icicles dripped from rotted plaster while tissue walls, brittle in the cold, fissured and cracked.

Victor, Timmy, and Stewart had volunteered to help me renovate this ruin and we struggled to equip it for human habitation. Every night after school the three boys arrived and set to work plastering, painting, sanding and varnishing floors, lugging coal, and building wardrobes.

They swore exhaustively, worked proficiently and, sensitive to my state of poverty, accepted only 'tea' as payment for their labours. It was a considerable wage in view of the vast quantities of food which they effortlessly packed away. They worked, and ate gaping holes into my heart and out through my shoulder blade.

Occasionally, Brian tried to help them. It was pathetic. Physically he was the strongest boy in the school and intellectually he was capable of attaining high academic standards. He was useless. School time was spent skulking about the animal pen growling,

'I'm in a fucking bad mood.'

Leaving no doubt as to the degree of foul mood, he shredded paper, bent axe handles, and clawed at the wall. Most of the students behaved in a violent manner when they were genuinely unable to control themselves, but Brian was bidding for attention and affection. By emulating his peers he hoped to win their esteem and respect, and when this failed, he increased his efforts to be truly disgusting.

Unlike most of the parents in our school, Brian's parents adored him and overwhelmed him with money, trips to the Continent, and expensive gifts, none of which improved his disposition. He skulked, glowered, and yearned for the companionship of other boys.

Intuitively, most of the children knew that Brian was gasping for affection and responded by tolerating his tantrums. I once asked Victor.

'But don't you like Brian?'

'Would you have a friend who's never happy?'

From time to time my trio of labourers allowed Brian to watch them at work on my flat, and one afternoon they found a job for him. All three boys were tradesmen's sons and from early childhood had been taught basic carpentry, electronics, and building. At home they had been required to help with the decorating, general repair, and wiring and were, by now, quite proficient. Brian was unable to change a light bulb.

'Brian, take these fucking doors off. We gotta plane the sods down before we can lay the carpet.'

Brian was delighted to find that they thought him capable of any work at all, and commenced on the bedroom door while I cooked 'tea' and the other three boys wired the sitting-room. The front door slammed shut. Stewart, Timmy, and Victor were swearing profoundly and splicing lead wire in the sitting-room.

'Who went out? Or came in?'

'Dunno. Thought it was you.'

'Well it wasn't.'

'Bri, maybe.'

'Where did he *go*? I'm supposed to be responsible for you while you're here.'

'Yeah.'

We skipped to the bedroom and reeled around the expanding hallway on a drunken merry-go-round. Catch the brass ring.

'Oh shit, Miss, just look at that.' I could scarcely see anything else.

'Wait till I get my hands on that chicken bastard.'

Brian had tried to unscrew the hinges on the door, broken two screwdrivers in the attempt, and apparently decided that the only way to remove the door was to rip it off. It now reclined against the wall, while one entire panel slowly detached itself and thudded to the floor. The door frame was split almost to the top, and chips of wood were scattered generously over the bedroom and hallway. Hinges and screws had disappeared entirely.

'Just wait till that fucker comes back. Just wait.'

'Never mind waiting. Find the hinges and screws.'

'What for. How're we going to get that door back on? That great, fat fucking sod.'

Brian had carefully buried the hinges and screws at the bottom of the litter bin. We drilled new holes, hung the mutilated door and found that it was a marvellous example of Future Art. The top sloped precariously and the panel, which we replaced with generous amounts of paste, flapped and banged on whim. Both frame and door had assumed a pronounced diagonal line. It was the last time Brian accompanied the boys to my flat.

Timmy was an affectionate boy who, until three years ago, had lived in the south of England. He was sent to us because he habitually stole. It was impossible to recall how many times he had been arrested, but I knew the items that stuck to his gummy fingers ranged from bicycles and mopeds to light bulbs whisked from the local buses. Just before he registered at St. Steven's his former headmaster sent a hand-written introductory letter:

'Tim has been a student in my school for the past three years and I have found him to be a most pleasant and affable boy. I am, of course, well aware of his history of stealing but am convinced that he is now beginning to cope with this problem. He does revert to crime occasionally but this is usually due to his desire to maintain a tough exterior. Timmy is insecure and basically soft but manages, by his lawless reputation and appearance, to sustain a position among his companions.

'Due to the fact that he is easily led, as well as the fact that his peers are involved with the police quite frequently, Timmy's attitude towards his problem would change should he be placed in Borstal. He would then welcome stealing as a means of winning admiration from fellow offenders and would, in my opinion, become quickly hardened to crime. As it is, his position at present is precarious.'

Months later I learned from Timmy's mother that when the boy was a baby, lead roofing had been dropped on his head from the top of a tenement. He had not been expected to live and had undergone several operations and many years in hospital before he was well enough to rejoin his family. Brain damage had never been ascertained but neurologists had stated that the boy was 'probably dispositionally and psychologically changed' after the accident. In contrast to the other six boys in his family, Timmy suffered increasingly violent temper tantrums and uncontrollable rages. His father, a successful carpenter, was unable to cope with Timmy's recurring skirmishes with the police and was bewildered by the boy's swaggering attitude towards authority. Tim's mother, a secretary, was too involved in her job and the care of the family to probe into the boy's behaviour patterns. Only when informed of a future court appearance did she give much attention to Tim's activities, in or out of school.

Timmy's IQ tested low-normal and he had little interest in, or talent for, academic subjects. Manual labour was a different matter altogether, for he felt confident in his ability to succeed in this type of undertaking. He lacked tenacity and the ability to concentrate, but willingly completed any task in which he felt competent. Like most of the students he was bored and unoccupied after school, looking forward with pleasure to the time-consuming work in my flat.

I asked him to change the lock on my front door and he agreed with alacrity. Swaggering home with me one afternoon he proceeded to remove the old-fashioned lock and handle with skill and rapidity, only to discover that he lacked the tools necessary to drill a round hole in the thick wood. Undaunted, he struggled to gouge the new hole, using a tiny screwdriver and a hammer. With each blow, and subsequent failure, his rage increased, scars turning scarlet, cheeks purple, throat straining, and spittle frothing down over the dimpled chin.

'You fucking cunt. Pissy arsed door . . .'

His voice slid up to an inflamed squeak, he flung the screwdriver to the floor and beat furiously upon the offensive door with the claw hammer. Chips of wood rained down in the frozen hallway and the door split.

Tears of frustration and anger iced his swollen face as he finally flung the hammer down the stairwell, shrieking,

'Pickles!'

It was the only word in his vocabulary which he considered truly obscene. Three renegade nerves ran along the peeling wallpaper and jumped into the stew, while I leaned on the cracked plaster and stuffed the crevices of my dissolving brain with sellotape. Timmy lay sobbing on the ancient wooden floor, scarred head resting against the crippled door. The giant door of wooden self-confidence slowly melted and trickled down the stairwell, dripping on to the pavement in muddy patches to be carefully skirted by respectable society.

Most of the information from these boys was gleaned, as in the case of Boysie, when they were engaged in some type of physical work. Raw bits of soul, which they offered to me on a broken chisel helped me to deal with them in school. Only when I understood their motives, conflicts, aspirations, and problems could I help each on an individual basis. This information was elicited slowly, and usually while working out of school. The concept of social conversation over a cup of tea was totally incomprehensible to these boys.

'Oi, Miss, what d'ya do at the parties you go to?' while putting up curtain rails.

'Oh, mostly talk.'

'*Talk!* What about?'

'Um. Oh, lots of things.'

'Well what?'

'Things I've done or other people have done, or plays we've seen or books. You know.'

'No I don't. Dontcha have punch-ups or nothing?'

'Of course not.'

'Fucking hell, sure glad I don't go to your parties.'

Free time was another mystery.

'What d'ya do when you're alone?'

Well, laddies, I first recuperate from school, which

takes about three hours, and then I spend the rest of the evening trying to determine whether or not I've passed over the line into insanity.

'Usually I read.'

'*Read*. When you don't have to? S'truth!'

Apparently they assumed that the six hundred books they had toted upstairs for me served no purpose other than of a very peculiar wall covering.

'That what you do with all them books?'

'That's right. I read them.'

'They're no good. You ain't got no comics.'

'So what else d'ya do?'

'Sometimes I sew. Or I write, or friends come to visit.'

'All you do is *talk* to them. You don't have no fucking fun at all!'

We stuffed cracks with rags, nailed windows shut, and pasted newspapers over broken panes, one of which boasted a bullet hole. Icicle-adorned air was trapped inside. I smoked and coughed. I prepared lessons in the bus every night in a humid soot-soaked vacuum, compounded of carbon dioxide, carbon monoxide, and carbon tetrachloride. I rang the Education Officer.

'No, Madam, the Department sees no reason to alter your standing and grant recognition.'

I contracted bronchitis at an inopportune time. I was out of food, paraffin, and money. Clutching my cigarettes and medicine, I donned all my winter clothes, wrapped up in a Moroccan rug and went to bed coughing. Una and Mabel arrived at six, swimming through the frost-infested air to my bed.

'We thought we should come and tell you that Seamus called a staff meeting this afternoon. He was wild.'

I coughed.

'Don't you want to know what he said?' Mabel glowed. If I said 'no' she would strangle on a clot of disappointment.

'What?'

'He's forbidden the kids to come here. None of them can come any more.'

'Why not? He suggested that they come in the first place.'

'He didn't think they'd become so attached to you, though. He was really ranting in the Staff Room, and went on about your morals. He said you're just a common streetwalker who bloody well can't teach. He said you have an untidy mind and an untidy life and he's running the school.'

'Right now my mind has an untidy cough.' I hacked twice and wished that I'd had the good sense to go into the streetwalking profession. 'So what does he want?'

'He wanted us to tell you.'

Catch the brass ring.

'Well tell him thanks for the solicitude and good wishes but I shall survive anyway and come back there to haunt him with ghoulish, untidy life.'

Mabel left, disappointed. Thriving on the troubles and difficulties of others, she probed ulcerated problems until they flared into a malignant, rotting pestilence. Her interest in my physical welfare waned when I failed to react to the rancid bait, and she stepped back into her web of torment to await a more responsive victim.

The bell chimed. Una opened the door to admit Timmy and Marrie, both of whom pushed past her into the icy hallway. From the bedroom I could hear the voices as they splintered the frozen air.

'Well, where is she then?'

'You both know you're not supposed to be here. I won't split on you, but if Sir hears about it he'll go spare.' Una's voice was pitched on a black note of fear and concern for the children.

'You just tell him to fuck off.'

They stormed into the bedroom.

'Oi, Miss, we come to take care'a you. How're ya feeling, then?'

For the next two weeks Marrie arrived every day after

school to cook my supper, change the bed, iron, clean, and wash. Sometimes she brought Timmy and a sibling or two and they scrubbed the floors, scoured the oven or took care of the laundry. I had no telephone, and every night she walked down the frozen road to the callbox to give progress reports to my doctor and friends. During my illness neither Seamus nor any of the staff, with the exception of Una, wrote or called in to see me.

'Marrie, leave that and I'll do it when I'm up.'

She and her younger brother Ted were sorting laundry one evening.

'Naw, Miss, fuck that. How're you gonna get well by yourself? You only just settled in here and don't even know nobody. All your mates live up town. You ain't even got no money, Miss, no money for *nothing*!'

Marrie's mother is from Saudi Arabia and her English father is serving a life sentence in prison. She has been raised on the premise that anything is permissible as long as you can get away with it. Her mother and seventeen other children and relatives lived in a two-room flat together with a young man who was shared by most of the female members of the group. Often Marrie arrived at school with tea leaves matted in her greasy blonde hair and damp tea stains soiling the tattered cardigan. 'My sister threw the teapot at Mum, but she missed, didn't she? Wait till I get her tonight, the fucking cow.'

Marrie's former Headmistress, a tough old lady of about sixty years and accustomed to dealing with the most difficult of girls, had sent an ultimatum to the Chief Education Officer: 'Either Marrie goes or I go. She's the most impossible uncontrollable student I have ever known.' So Marrie came to us.

This was probably the first time in her fourteen years that she had behaved in an unselfish manner, and yet in so acting she was now breaking a school law.

'Marrie, you'll get into trouble. You aren't supposed to be here.'

'That old git can go get stuffed. He's just spiteful and jealous. Piss on him. I'll get my Dad after him, won't I?'

After a two-week absence I returned to school, coughing my way down the corridor past rows of gloating balloons wearing expressions of anticipation. They saluted. I beat upon Seamus' office door with my cough.

'I'm back, Seamus. I understand that there was some trouble while I was away. What's the problem?'

'Sure you should be back? You look like hell.'

'Probably, but what was all this about?'

'Now, now, it's all blown over. I received some complaints from the parents, but I managed to calm them down.'

'What parents? The only children who come to my flat are Timmy, Stewart, Victor, and Marrie. I know those parents very well and have drinks and tea with them.'

This information was a shock for which he was totally unprepared. He began to sharpen a fang on one gold inlaid cuff link.

'I want to know who complained, and what it was about.'

'That's confidential. I can't possibly tell you.'

Nothing here was ever confidential. Seamus had seen, in my illness, the opportunity to play a dramatic role, thickening the clouds of tension and instability. The hapless children were confused and bewildered. They had been castigated for committing criminal offences and equally chastised for unselfishly helping a teacher in need. They were crushed, subdued, convinced of their own congenital worthlessness. Seamus strode about the stage, shaking the curtains of instability.

'Seamus. I want to *know*!'

'We'll just forget it. I want you to forget all about it. I need you here. You're doing very well, and you know that I'll be the first one to tell you if you aren't. I don't know what Una told you but I would never say anything about you when you aren't here . . .'

I turned towards the door, feeling quite ill.

'I'll stay, Seamus, because I like the children.'

The masks slid slowly down and were replaced by teacher faces as I opened his office door.

I revolved down the hallway.

Back to class.

CHAPTER THIRTEEN

I COUGHED and tried to contain Gaylord, whose violence had not diminished during my absence.

'If you stab Tina with that pencil one more time, Gaylord, I'm going to give you bronchitis.'

Apparently he thought that the ailment was an American-type toy, for he renewed his attack on Tina, demanding that I fulfil my promise.

'Give me the bronchitis.'

'Gaylord, *stop that*. Tina, run to the office. Don't just stand there, *run*. Gaylord, give me the pencils.'

He chucked them at my head.

'I want the bronchitis. Give me the bronchitis.'

In desperation I ran to the woods, clawed at the packed earth, and captured a tiny newt which was presented to Gaylord.

'This, Gaylord, is a rare type of animal called a bronchitis.'

He ate the newt.

Timmy's sister was to be married, and his Mum, one of the alleged complainants, invited me to the wedding. All the other guests were Welsh or Cockney, and I failed to communicate with either species, although I felt that I might be grasping a few language fundamentals when I correctly translated 'up the apples and pears'. The bride was lovely, the groom nervous, and after the wedding we all retired to an empty room over the local pub and got pissed to the sounds of a pop group emanating from a record player. They were warbling something about the sun, a subject which I found intriguing, particularly since I hadn't seen this celestial body for the last two years. Guests, record player, and several crates of beer drifted to Timmy's house in the early morning. Settling into a corner with a row of opened beers close to hand I guzzled, listening to the pop group describing the strange, foreign object in the sky. Hazily I speculated on the remote possibility of actually seeing the sun again. Next morning I found myself neatly folded up on a sofa, together with four of Timmy's aunts from Wales. I discovered that I had grown hair in my mouth and, while trying to scrape it out, suddenly realized that my eyes had been replaced by two peeling red discs that tore into the flesh of my face. With shaking hand I stuck on my false lashes, one of which pointed stiffly at the ceiling. The other curled under, sweeping the rough surface of my red, marbled eye with every blink. I looked for my contact lenses and failed to find the left one. Frantically I searched my bag, hunted on the sofa, under the sofa and then microscopically inspected my pockets. Timmy, his aunts and siblings joined me, dropping to all fours and sweeping every inch of the house with hungover hands in search of one glittering green contact lens. After an hour the hunt stopped. Resigned to blindness of the left eye until I could scrape together enough money for a lens I took out my lipstick and prepared to walk home through the common in my silver sandals and whisky-stained velvet dress. Jerking the gold top from my lipstick case I pushed up the greasy stick of coloured stain and opened my mouth. I closed my mouth. There, nestling comfortably on the top of my Coral Fire lip grease, was the contact lens. It winked maliciously. I jabbed it into my eye, found my dignity and stuffed it into my left ear, wishing that Seamus could see my untidy life at this moment.

Four nights later Timmy rang my bell. His acne was livid and his face green as he tramped into the kitchen and flopped in a chair. Absently he kicked at a crack in the lino and stared at a puddle of water under the sink. He refused to look at me.

'Want some coffee?'

'Yeah.'

'What's the matter?'

'I've got sticky fingers again.'

'I can see that, but what have they stuck to now?'

'A moped.'

'Marvellous. Where is it?'

'Drove it over the tip, didn't I, I rode the bugger around for about an hour first.'

That damned tip again. Apparently all the hot vehicles in the city were deposited in this favoured spot. As the police did not patrol the area, it was also a gathering place for the students during holidays and after school. Scrabbling through heaps of refuse, they claimed any machine still in working order and, for a few hours, drove them along the paths in the dump. Before leaving, the children dismantled the vehicles, removing any saleable items for presentation to the local junk dealer. Most of the children received no spending money from home, but never lacked king-size cigarettes, thanks to the financial assistance of the tip.

'You'd better go and get it, Timmy, and put it back.'

'Go get it? Fucking hell, it won't run now, will it? I drove it over the edge. Anyway, it don't belong to nobody. Its been parked in that street for weeks.'

'Don't be so stupid, of course someone owns it. They

just park it in the same place every night. You'll have to ask someone to help you put it back before the owner reports it stolen.'

He sat, unmoving, tracing his scars with one grimy finger.

'I mean move now.'

'You gonna tell Sir?'

'Naturally, Timmy, I have to tell him. Since I'm not calling the law I'm accessory to a felony, and if the police see you with that moped I'll be in the nick too. Seamus has to know about it in case he's short of a teacher in the morning. I want you to get the number from it and then come back here. After you've put it back.'

'You gonna tell my Mum?'

'No, why should I?'

'Well, don't. She'll knock the crap out of me.'

He didn't care if I knew, if Seamus knew, or even if the law found out, but for God's sake don't tell Mum.

'Gotta tanner, Miss? I'm skint.'

I took sixpence from my bag and gave it to the disconsolate boy.

'And Timmy, come back here after you make the phone call, please. Without sticking to anything else.'

'Yeah, yeah.'

He shuffled off to the phonebox and rang Brian who was thrilled to be selected as an accomplice in this exciting adventure. He promised to join Timmy at my flat immediately, and Tim shuffled back to wait. We sat in silence, drinking coffee and smoking countless cigarettes, waiting. Time, always undependable, ran in reverse. The cigarettes stank, skin floated on the coffee, and my hands left wet palm prints on the cold air. The bell rang, and the boys set off for the tip. I set off for the callbox and rang Seamus.

'I knew this is what would happen if Timmy went over there. It's why I can't have the boys paying visits to your flat.'

Fagan lives.

'Seamus, he came afterwards, he didn't ask my permission. I'm just telling you what I've done about it.'

'Um, ahem, yes. Yes. I'll ring one of my friends on the force and fix it. Let me know when the boys come back.'

He spent a great deal of time in his Club cultivating the friendship of a few plainclothes detectives in the area. Grateful for the entertainment and thirsty for more, these officers of the law were indispensable in incidents such as this one.

Three thousand hours and three hundred cigarettes later the bell rang. I dried my clammy hands, nailed my nerves into place and prepared to greet the police. It was Timmy and Brian.

'Put it back, didn't we?'

'Did you get the number?'

'No, forgot it, didn't I?'

'Oh God! Well, never mind. Don't go back for it now.'

'We saw the Bill.'

'Fine. Did they see you?'

'No, we hid in the bushes. Some old git was looking out of the window but he didn't do nothing.'

'Timmy, I wish you could understand that Brian and I are both accessories when you do things like this.'

'I wouldn't 'ave split on you. Anyway, you're always an accessory, aren'tcha?'

'Go home.'

'You ain't cross are you, Miss?'

'No. See you in the morning.'

'If you're lucky.'

Some luck.

CHAPTER FOURTEEN

All the students at St. Steven's were certified 'maladjusted', and many of them were handicapped and subnormal as well. Any child with multiple inadequacies was sent to us if maladjustment was included in the defects.

Allen Cunningham's reason for admission was 'poor visuo-motor co-ordination and disturbed behaviour. Suspected brain damage'. Allen was chubby and clumsy, unable to move or speak properly. The vast majority of his time was spent compulsively twiddling with string or tape while grimacing and singing to himself. He was unable to hold a pencil, and made abortive attempts to write academic lessons on the blackboard with a large piece of chalk. Craft class was a disaster resulting in mutilated fingers, paint-caked clothing and broken equipment. Completely unco-ordinated and unsuccessful in PT, the lesson always terminated with Allen screaming hysterically in rage and frustration. Because he was unable to join in any school activity, all trace of self-confidence vanished, and he refused to attempt the simplest exercise. The twiddling increased. We took away his string and tape and he found more in the trash bins, in the woods, under the desks. In the event of failure, rubber bands or long pieces of grass served remarkably well as substitutes.

I had forgotten that it was my day on duty. I usually forgot. 'Selective forgetting', Seamus called it. On duty days one patrolled the grounds and school in fragmented bits, searching with two million eyes for trouble trying to crawl from the mousehole. Trouble, however, usually emerged from a tiny, undetected cavity while one was kicking viciously and ineffectually at an empty cavern.

I was slumped in the Staff Room, prying scum from the top of my coffee. A pair of crossed eyes peered over the window ledge and Philip squeaked:

'Oi, Allen's cut his hand, hasn't he?'

Mabel pawed the floor in happy anticipation.

'Where is he?'

'Locked in the shed, Miss.'

'The shed?'

'Yeah, Miss.'

'Who's on duty?'

An invisible boot connected with my bottom and lifted me out of the straight-back-chair.

'Oh Jesus. Me. I'm sorry, I forgot again.'

Faces were painted with smirks as I shot through the doorway and around the corner of the school.

As part of Seamus' outdoor-work therapy, he had unpredictably ordered construction of this shed a few days earlier. A building firm had generously donated the defective material and Seamus announced, while buffing his glistening nails, that the finished shed would be used to house the children's Wellington boots. As children and staff toiled to erect the tiny shack, Seamus ordered destruction of the asbestos roof. Confused and discouraged by the certainty that razing would follow construction of the now useless building, the children laboured on, clinging to familiar clots of instability. Under the supervision of a rubber puppet, windows had been put in place and, for some indecipherable reason, newspaper pasted over the glass.

Today one of the students had locked Allen inside the roofless shack, knowing that the boy became hysterical at the slightest provocation. As was expected, he screamed, cried, and begged for release, while the other children danced excitedly around the shed. Panic stricken, Allen stuck his arm through the newspaper shrouded pane. 'Sales and Wants' cracked and shattered as Allen dragged his arm back inside, ripping baby flesh on the features editor and tearing arteries on 'Births and Deaths'. I skidded to the shed and was tugged round the corner of Abel's soothing tones:

'Don't worry, Allen, we'll have you out in a second. It's all right. You'll be all right.'

He frantically tore the remaining paper-coated glass from the window.

'There, Al, I'm right here. I'll get you out. No, no, don't cry.'

Abel. Of all the children at school Abel was the first to vanish in the face of trouble. He was usually Timmy's partner in crime, but it was always Timmy who was caught. It was apparently impossible to reach Abel through fear, kindness, or love and he was the only student whom the entire staff felt might profit by a term in Borstal. He had lost five part-time jobs, either through dipping into the till or spewing a mouthful of garbage at a customer. Once he had run away from home, being tracked down by Brian and Stewart, and brought to my flat.

'Help him, Miss.'

Help him. I didn't know how. I sent him home.

He ripped out the last chunk of glass and reached over a bloodied *Sports News*.

'Come on, Al. Here I'll lift you out. That's it. Careful, no, no, don't scream. That's it.'

He carried Allen, holding the shredded arm high to stem the spurt of blood. Streaked with rust he rode to the hospital, soothing and cradling the hysterical child.

That arm. Strings of flesh and fat squirting streams of coloured corpuscles. Oozing black tears I wandered into the school, past balloons of triumph, past Gaylord stabbing Tina with a compass, past Brian ripping radiators from the wall. Seamus' eyes, surrounded by etched ochre wrinkles, absorbed the light. Enraged, he dipped into the pus pot and switched on the tannoy.

'Everyone in the hall – it's now.'

Polishing a diamond ring on his linen handkerchief he slithered on stage, prepared for a gala performance.

I'm a real lousy teacher.

CHAPTER FIFTEEN

THE year's shortest term had finally come to an end. My blistered nerves lay carefully coiled inside a jar of embalming jelly while I dipped my sullied mind into a bucket of bleach.

Once more we packed into the Staff Room, again waiting for notice of schedule changes. Seamus handed out the mimeographed sheets.

'Now this term I'm going to try something completely different. We really need an adequate Staff Room, so I'm going to create space for one. I've eliminated one of the classes entirely, and we will use Frank's room for the new Staff Room. Frank, you take your class in the Hall. All classes will be larger and Conor, you'll have no class.'

Ha. I must have been promoted to assistant caretaker.

'I'm turning the air-raid shelter into a craft room and you'll be our new art and craft teacher. As such, you'll have all the classes for one hour every day.'

Life is so kind. I have the opportunity to teach art without paper and craft without any supplies.

'With what do I teach?'

'Damn it, we have plenty of lino cutters and bits of old lino. I've ordered clay, and we have a kiln, so you can concentrate on pottery. Go in and see what else's there.'

'Sir!'

I pushed out and trotted to the air-raid shelter. Holy Moses, I don't believe it. The room was about ten feet square with a cement partition down the centre. Just perfect. When I'm in one half of the room I can't see the kids on the other side. For this I can't wait.

The walls were thick, whitewashed brick, and the floors bare cement. There were no windows or ventilators, no heat, and only one door which opened not outdoors, but into Una's classroom. There were no cupboards, no sink and, mercifully, no tannoy. Clammy cold seeped from moist brick walls, coagulated on the chilly cement floor. Slippery chill drizzled on to the sole neon light and slid down a beam on to my feet.

Behind me, Seamus picked his way carefully into the shelter, flicking lint and frozen crystals from his mohair suit. He rested delicately against the kiln, after first dusting it languidly with a silk handkerchief.

'There's a lot of clay arriving this week. I'll have a sink put in and . . .'

'When?'

'Uh? Oh, you know. I have other priorities.'

'How about getting some air in here?'

'Yes, yes. Air. Well, you don't really need that right away.'

'Correct. One thing I do not need is air.

'I can't manage without water, Seamus. You said pottery and one does need water for that.'

'Oh no problem. No problem at all. We have plenty of plastic buckets. Just have each class fill all the buckets at the beginning of the hour and empty them at the end. And for God's sake try and keep it tidy.'

We tried. Getting water to the room necessitated a constant chain of children trekking through Una's classroom, through the hall, down the corridor and out of the front door to the tap. Classes in session were interrupted as my artists fetched and dumped water, slopping it in generous amounts through the school. Red clay coated every wall and door between the air-raid shelter and the tap. Antiquated lavatory drains were continually blocked, and dusty red hand-prints were to be found on almost every window.

Seamus' voice grated over the tannoy.

'All right! Everybody get this school cleaned up. I want these floors and walls scrubbed and if I find red clay anywhere you'll all stay after hours and do it again. I don't have to be home until nine tonight. You may live like damned pigs at home but I want this school clean. I have visitors coming.'

We scrubbed, cleaned, and washed. Seamus inspected, smoothing the steel clocks above his bony face as we leaned, panting and sweating, against the immaculate wall.

'Right. It's a bloody bad job but I'll pass it this time. Now get into those toilets and get busy. I don't know how you can use filthy holes like that. Damned animals.'

Drawing back with distaste he slithered into his office. We slumped, gathering strength for the coming attack on the loos.

Marrie screamed,

'I ain't cleaning no pissy bog-hole. I come here to learn and I ain't gonna do no fucking cleaner's work. That bastard can just get stuffed. Wait'll I tell my Dad.'

'Oh hush, Marrie and go get the disinfectant. I don't know about you but I want to finish this before nine tonight, so let's get busy.'

The lavatories evidently had not seen a cleaner's hand in many years. We scraped at dirt ingrained in windowsills, scoured stains in the urinals and scrubbed filthy toilets. We washed walls, windows and floors, poured disinfectant liberally over the room and began again.

We finished at five. Exhausted and disgruntled the students gathered in the hall for dismissal, muttering resentfully.

'My old school had a cleaner. We never had to do no work like this.'

'Sod that, we got a cleaner here but he ain't doing nothing.'

Marrie screeched,

'I'm not cleaning that fucking bog again. He can get stuffed.'

Silence blanketed the room, stifling the protestations as Seamus undulated through the doorway, rearranging the silk handkerchief in his breast pocket. Taking a gold lighter from one pocket he tapped polished nails lightly on the metal as he surveyed the wordless room.

'It's an improvement but it's not good enough. First thing tomorrow morning I want all of you in overalls and Wellingtons ready to work! We'll give this school a good cleaning and then I want you all straight into your classes. And if you can't keep the school tidy we'll do this every morning for the rest of the term. Damned pigs! Dismissed!'

Two days later the walls were caked, the drains blocked and the windows bore handprints in dusty red clay.

We worked with clay although we had no sculpture tools, no wire, no glazes, and no brushes. We made slip glazes, and the students decorated in two colours, using sticks in place of brushes. Nails, plastic spoons, and twigs replaced necessary tools. Daily we fired clay creations in the kiln, raising the room temperature to over one hundred degrees. We sculpted in granite and chalk, substituting sandpaper and nails for the proper implements. Dust and grit clogged the clammy air, and I began to cough again. The children began to cough. We made lino-cuts on strips of discarded floor linoleum and used house paint from the caretaker's hut for printing. We made constructions from paper drinking straws, mobiles from coat hangers, papier mâché wall hangings from newspaper, and glass and cement mosaics from bottles which I again reluctantly collected.

'Seamus, I need some turps.'

'Well, there's no money for unnecessary items.'

'The children are printing with oil base house paint and turps are necessary.'

'You've got a problem.'

I bought turps, coloured paper and Sellotape. We worked and we liked it.

I sloshed water on to lino-topped tables, transforming

the dried clay to dull red mud. My attempt to mop up the muddy surface resulted in a dirty red streaked lino. I poured fresh water on to the table and tried to clean the lino.

The kiln was turned on and the heat was overpowering. Humidity gathered and dripped from the ceiling while rivulets of water coursed down the walls. The temperature rose to a stifling one hundred degrees and continued to climb. Perspiration ran into my eyes, down my back and down my legs. My drenched clothes clung to me in sodden folds as I scrubbed at the tables.

Timmy peeped around the partition, then ducked back.

'Oi, Stew, she's here.'

Timmy shuffled around the corner, followed by Stewart who promptly hoisted himself to a sitting position on a red-streaked table.

'Watcha, Miss. S'truth! Ain't it hot in here! Is it like this where you come from?'

'Not quite. I don't come from the Congo, you know. Please get off the table, Stew, I can't clean it with you sitting there.'

Stewart swung his legs, settling more comfortably on to the clay-covered surface, while Timmy picked up a hammer and flailed idly at the wall.

'What's the Congo?'

'I'll show it to you on the map later. For God's sake, *stop that banging*! I know you don't believe it but these walls are quite capable of falling down. If you want something to do you can try helping me out with this.'

Timmy threw the hammer on to the concrete floor and coughed.

'Oi, Miss, what d'ya think about sex before marriage?'

Perhaps they had tried to select the most devastating time and place for serious discussion. They had succeeded. My mind began to jiggle and swim and one nerve over my eyebrow commenced ticking. I set to work on another table.

'Think about it? That's not very clear. What do you mean?'

'Do you think it's all right? Ya know, is it O.K. to have sex before you're married?'

'Well, of course, I think it's all right, depending upon the other person. I think it's very unwise to sleep around, but if you really love someone, or think you do, it's part of knowing them. After all, marriage is not just a licence for sex.'

Stewart stopped swinging his legs.

'My sister got married because she was up the spout.'

'Stew, if you don't know anything about contraception you shouldn't be talking about sex.'

'What's contraception?'

'Birth control.'

'Oh.' He began to swing his legs again.

'Ya think sex before marriage is O.K., then? With just one person.'

'Timmy, you must know someone very, very well in many ways before you marry. The desire for sex should not be a reason for marriage.'

'Miss MacMichael.'

Seamus' hoarse voice filled the steamy shelter. Stewart slid from the table and fled around the corner with Timmy, as the Headmaster, glowering, descended upon me.

'What in the hell do you think you're here for? To teach these kids immorality? I heard that crap you were handing Timmy and Stewart. Sex education is not included in our curriculum because I don't think you or anyone else is qualified to teach it. And *you*, Miss MacMichael, are *not* paid to encourage promiscuity.'

His voice had risen to a thunderous bellow. I gazed at the gaunt face. Transparent skin, stretched taut over the cheek-bones, was furrowed by dark wrinkles. Trembling with rage, he knotted one stringy claw around the broom handle. Even in the oppressive heat of the shelter his skin was dry and cool like that of any reptile.

'Seamus, I am well acquainted with the advice handed to these children. At home, at school, at any club they hear sermons about purity until marriage. These kids have been screwing since they were ten and their sex is usually indiscriminate. Just about anyone will do for them. Telling them the same old story won't influence them at all. It's too damned late. They asked *my* personal opinion, they didn't ask me to parrot the usual song and dance. They can smell hedging and lying, you know that. I *gave* them *my* opinion.'

Unconsciously, Seamus dusted at the lapel of his immaculate jacket. His eyes gleamed with maniacal fury, and the cords in his neck jerked as he leaned towards me.

'You're not only a rotten teacher, you're immoral! I've said it before and I'll say it now; you are untidy, inefficient and you lead a lascivious life. Your job is to tell these girls to get rings on their fingers, and the boys to get respectably married. You remember this, Conor, I can have you out of this school in five minutes and I'll do it if there is one more incident like this. Whenever you feel the urge to make a speech you make one about rings. Don't hand me any crap about the kids' sex life at present. What they do out of this school is not my concern, but in my school I want them to think about wedding rings. Nothing else!'

Shaking, Seamus slithered from the shelter. His retreating figure wavered in the increasing heat and a solitary drop of water fell from the ceiling to mark one spotless shoulder. Outside I could hear hysterical screams as Gaylord, encouraged by Marrie, threw the caretaker's axe at Tina.

Numbly, I began to scrub the caked tables.

Gaylord was with me for only one hour each day, during which time he sculpted in clay. Most of his pottery creations were enormous in size and ranged, in subject matter, from elephants and birds to phallic symbols. One morning he scooped clay from the bin, retired to the farthest corner of the room, and worked furtively throughout the hour. At the end of the lesson he wrapped the unseen artistic product in his overall and marched from the air-raid shelter. Finding this behaviour slightly more odd than usual I followed him. He spread the overall out underneath one of the prefab classrooms, carefully arranging the unrevealed creation on top, and strode away. I bent to look. He had spent the morning making hundreds of tiny clay pellets for his catapult. God. I squashed them into a massive ball and returned the clay to the bin. That afternoon I faced a glowering Gaylord.

'Where's my beads?'

'They're gone, Gaylord. You know you can't have those in school.'

'Want my beads.'

'Well, they're gone now.'

'Jus' you wait, you fucker. I'll get you. I want my beads.'

He drew one sinewy arm back and hit me in the chest. I collapsed on the floor. Brian seized Gaylord, attempting to pinion his arms, and the deranged boy bit Brian's arm to the bone.

I writhed on the floor and gasped.

'Take him to Seamus, Brian.'

Brian pulled and dragged Gaylord through the hall, while the latter ripped down the curtains, kicked Timmy in the crutch, and bit Brian's other arm. Wrenching free at last he whirled towards Una, dropped to a crouch and pointed two stiff index fingers at her eyes.

'I'm gonna squash your eyes,' he growled, and sped towards her. Screaming in terror Una fled through the school towards Seamus' office with Gaylord in pursuit.

Stewart helped me up to a limp squat and I dragged along after them, clutching my painful bosom.

Still screaming, Una flung open the door of Seamus' office, sped across the room and jumped into his lap. A stunning woman was seated in the visitors' chair and, unfortunately, she wore a strand of pearls. While Una clung to Seamus' corded neck, her face buried in white silk, Gaylord pounced on the visitor, toppled her from the chair and tugged at the pearls, snarling.

'Want the beads.'

They rolled about on the office floor, guest pulling at her skirt and Gaylord pulling on the pearl necklace. Seamus uncoiled, flicking at Una and shouting.

'What the hell is this? Get out of here, Una, can't you see that I have a visitor? Gaylord, man, damn it, stop that! Gaylord, get up!'

He pulled Gaylord up, breaking the strand of pearls. Gaylord spat upon Seamus' new grey flannel suit.

'Fuck off. Jus' you wait.'

Seamus threw cold water on the boy, then struck him repeatedly about the head. Gaylord sat down crying, brown hands covering his face, while watching us with blank, sightless eyes.

The titian-haired guest was crawling about the floor, searching for her jewellery. Seamus helped her to her feet and she stood arranging torn clothing, disordered hair and smeared lipstick.

'Dr. Grimsby! Hello. I didn't know you were coming this afternoon.' Una was pasted to the wall opposite Gaylord, and now greeted the guest, Dr. Grimsby, Senior Educational Psychiatrist.

'Una, Miss MacMichael. How nice. Yes, I have an appointment with Mr. O'Shea to discuss Gaylord's future.' She edged closer to the door, averting her eyes from the boy who sat watching us through a slit in two separated fingers.

Seamus smoothed the silk shirt and picked at a trace of

lipstick on the flannel shoulder. Taking out his linen handkerchief he patted delicately at the mauve wrinkles that fissured his scaley face. Glancing into the mirror over the washbasin he adjusted the vents in his jacket and turned to us.

'Will you two get back to your classes? What the bloody hell are *you* doing here, Conor? Can't anyone around here teach? Get out!'

'Now, Dr. Grimsby, this is an example of teachers who are unable to control. You have no idea of the difficulties I have here with the staff. Gaylord has improved tremendously, of course. This was very unfortunate but . . .'

Gaylord snarled, 'Want my beads.'

Stewart helped me back to the shelter.

'You all right, Miss?'

'Um. I just lost my left tit.'

'Doesn't look like it to me.'

'So I'm not looking.'

'Who started him off this time, Miss?'

Seamus' brainwashing was successful. The children thought Gaylord incapable of irrational behaviour unless intolerably goaded.

'Stewart, no one started him. He's just not right.'

'Well he ain't stupid, is he?'

'That has nothing to do with mental health, Stewart. Some totally insane people are very intelligent. You don't have to be a moron to be mentally very, very ill.'

Stewart was silent, picking at an angry cut on his forearm. He had begun to slash himself again, an indication that tension was building and would soon culminate in an outburst of violence. This usually took the form of arson or vandalism.

'Look, Stewart, it's difficult to explain this to you, but Gaylord doesn't know the difference between right and wrong. He has no relationships with any other human beings, nor can he relate to himself. The rest of you all do some very odd things. That's why you're here. You go spare, you misbehave, you get into trouble with the law, but you always know that whatever you do will have some consequences. You may refuse to study because you want my attention, or you may study hard because you want to please me. You break in and you know that you'll be sent down if the police catch you. You're aware of what you are doing and you usually have at least a vague idea of the result, although you may not know why you are doing a particular thing. Gaylord is completely unaware of any consequences relating to his actions, and often is unaware of the actions themselves.'

Stewart was silent.

'Stew, do you remember the time Gaylord locked himself in the staff loo?'

'Yeah.'

One morning Gaylord, in a sudden fit of violence, had thrown all the books down from the hall bookcase, ripped the covers of most of them and then vaulted down the corridor to lock himself in the staff lavatory. We pleaded, we bribed him with chocolates, Seamus threatened immediate belting, all of which brought no response of any kind. We took a ladder to the outside of the lavatory, climbed up and looked over the top of the window. Gaylord was standing in the centre of the room, sightless eyes turned in upon the warp and woof of a satin mind, giggling to himself. Seamus turned the hose on him from over the window top while Boysie and Stewart broke down the door.

'Don't you see, Stew, that Gaylord was totally unaware of the commotion and really didn't know that he had caused any trouble. Any of you might have done the same thing, but you would have known what you were doing and what the result would be.'

'Yeah, I guess.'

I did not feel that I had been very successful.

'Come on, Mr. Robertson, and help me clean up this room.'

He slid from the table top, jammed his hands into the pockets of his jeans and spat the matchstick on the floor.

'Don't call me Robertson. Ever!'

'For God's sake why not? It's your name.'

'It's my father's name.'

Before Stewart was born his parents had cohabited for several years in apparent harmony, producing two daughters. Shortly before the boy's birth they had married and, for some obscure reason, the father disappeared about a month later. Stewart was placed in a nursery when a few days old. At a year he was removed to a foster home for a short period, and then placed in another nursery. Life, for Stewart, consisted of a series of strange nurseries and foster homes until his eighth birthday when he was reunited with his mother and sisters. Not surprisingly, he was certified maladjusted at six years, entered a special school, and has been in special education ever since. In concise, clinical language the psychiatrist reported, 'Stewart is still severely deprived as a result of lack of affection and security through the early years'. Described, in as few words as possible, emotional starvation.

Having no hobbies, belonging to no clubs, Stewart's free time was spent roaming the streets, and he was often involved in vandalism, arson, and breaking and entering. Highly skilled in the latter craft, he was capable of entering any building at will. I had watched him scale sheer brick walls, silently pry open a locked window, and disappear inside. I had also seen him deftly pick a variety of locks, including one removed from a safe, using a piece of wire and a table knife. He owned a substantial variety of locks and keys which were used for the purpose of practice, and he spent long hours both in and out of school, taking the locks apart, trying various keys, fiddling with wire and noting the time required to open each type of lock. I had originally asked Stewart, not Timmy, to replace my front door lock.

'No, Miss.'

'Why not? You're good with locks.'

'I'm good at getting the buggers open, but I don't know how to put them on doors.'

Unlike most boys who were convicted of breaking and entering, Stewart never stole from the premises once he was inside. Boysie once said,

'Fucking stupid, ain't it, Miss? He goes to all that trouble and all he does is look around. That ain't what I'd do, is it?'

No, it's not.

Stewart's obsession with the interiors of homes and buildings probably stemmed from his own appalling home life. A recent report from a welfare worker described the family's slum dwelling:

'The family's housing conditions are very bad, and except for Mark Gorman, are the worst of any child enrolled in the school. Mrs. Robertson, Stewart, and his three sisters share one bedroom, while there is no bathroom or inside lavatory. Heating is by coal and, as there is no storage space for this fuel, it is kept in the entry hall. Mrs. Robertson has been told that it will be at least five years before the family can be rehoused.'

Until he was twelve years of age, Mrs. Robertson had never discussed her husband with Stewart, but managed to convey the impression that his father was away and would return at any moment. Every day after school Stewart went to the railway station, waiting for his father who never came home, and never would come home. Finally, a clinic worker asked Mrs. Robertson if she would attempt to enlighten the boy regarding his father's desertion, and Mrs. Robertson agreed to try and broach the subject within the next few months. Later, the clinic worker and Stewart discussed his father's disappearance for the first time and Stew said that his paternal parent had drowned. The worker made the following astute note during this interview:

'We discussed Stewart's father and the boy maintains that Mr. Robertson drowned. Is this one of Stewart's phantasies or did Mrs. Robertson or his sisters tell him this? During the time Stewart was fostered out Mrs. Robertson gave birth to another daughter. Did Mr. Robertson return at this time? How many of the children are the offspring of Stewart's father? Stewart frequently attempts to throttle and/or drown other boys (e.g. Lawrence L. in 1966, P.B., Lewis, Matthew, etc.): what is the connection between his father's disappearance and these actions? At some time, discover:

1. Stewart's feelings towards his father;
2. What happened to Stewart and also to his family in the early years when they were separated;
3. What happened to Mr. Robertson after he deserted and whether, in fact, he returned.

Caseworkers in the borough were at a premium, the clinic understaffed, and turnover of personnel high. Stewart's case was sporadically probed by various overworked clinic workers, all of whom lacked both the time and the tenacity necessary to delve deeply into the boy's past and present problems. None of the above questions has ever been answered.

At about this time Stewart had received a serious scalp wound while he and several contemporaries were demolishing the local pub into which they had broken. Stew was left with a nasty scar of which he was exceedingly proud, and has worn his hair short since that time in order to exhibit the wound to full advantage.

A few years ago the borough psychiatrist had said of Stewart:

'This is the most active child I have ever seen. I can't see how any contact can be made with him at all.'

I had no difficulty making contact with Stewart but it was, at times, incredibly frustrating. He would never answer a direct question, and it was impossible to force information from him. Choosing the most improbable times, he dropped vital information. I was constantly alert and tuned to receive both oblique references and bold statements mumbled in passing by the boy. Stewart never repeated himself and the words, if first missed, were lost for ever.

He was very popular with the other students but shirked the responsibility of leadership, remaining content with the power of influence. Emotion, rather than reason, governed his ideas of justice and retribution.

'All right, then Stewart James. Help me.'

He did.

In his customary stiff-gaited manner Gaylord entered, munching a biscuit. All trace of the recent violence had evaporated, and he stood, silently staring.

'Where's my elephant?'

Earlier in the week he had created a giant clay elephant.

'Over there.'

'Wanna paint it. I said I wanna paint it, you bitch.'

'All right. We have some new colours that Sir just bought for us. Which one do you want for your elephant?'

'Red. I said red!'

'Yes, I heard you. No, Gaylord, don't mix it yourself, you're using the enamels. Here, I'll do it and then you can paint the elephant.'

For most of the next hour Gaylord painted, meticulously coating the animal with too much glaze. He painted inside the nostrils, inside the trunk, inside the ears, applied an unnecessary fourth coat to the body, and announced that he had finished.

'Wanna take it home.'

'Not now, Gaylord. No, *listen* to me.' He had tensed for another fit. 'See how it comes off on my hands? We'll cook it in the kiln tomorrow and it will be lovely and shiny. You don't want dirty glaze powder on your jumper do you? Tomorrow then.'

'Cook it?'

He giggled, put stiff brown hands over his face and stalked from the room, grinding biscuit crumbs into his woolly hair. Stewart and I continued to clean the room.

CHAPTER SIXTEEN

THE tannoy drew to attention. 'I wanted everyone in a swimming costume and I want you to line up outside in pairs. Now.'

We were already late for the weekly swimming lesson in the local baths. A straggly row began to form as students meandered out of the front door, breaking into a trot as they glimpsed Seamus by the gate. Marrie and Greta appeared in cotton dresses, and Seamus glided back from the fencing, lavender wrinkles slipping into place between the strings of his forehead.

'I said *everyone* in a swimming costume.'

'I forgot mine.'

'Mine's ugly.'

'I'll give you three minutes to find the costumes and put them on. At the end of that time you will go swimming as you are. If you happen to be naked at the end of three minutes you will swim in the nude.'

Three minutes later they appeared in bathing costumes, Seamus retired to his office and secretary, and we climbed on the coach. As we turned into the High Street Gaylord jumped from his seat, ran down the aisle, and throttled the driver, mumbling,

'Want my catapult and beads.'

The coach veered over the edge of the pavement and stopped, resting lightly against a brick building, as the driver clawed at Gaylord's hands. We pried the boy away and dragged him back down the aisle.

'He doesn't have your beads, Gaylord.'

Mabel folded over the back of a seat, gasping for air, as he hit her in the stomach. Brian pushed down the aisle and kicked Gaylord in the small of the back as Stewart hit him on the side of the head. Spreading him on the aisle, Brian sat on Gaylord's shoulders and Stewart on his bum, while the driver massaged his swollen throat. The engine started, and our coach backed away from the brick building and an army of curious housewives with prams that had gathered to watch. Buy your tickets, ladies, and see the show.

I sat, ignoring the children who jostled one another in the ribs, punched viciously between the seats, and conducted hair-pulling contests over the seat tops. Looking out of the window of my cage the grass and trees rolled into a sun-speckled, green ball that wavered and blurred into indistinct, soothing tones. My eyes prickled and stung, salty water sheeted over my contact lenses, and I blinked blindly. A wad of hopelessness built in my throat, and I couldn't swallow.

In front of me Marrie screamed:

'Oi, Miss, whatsa matter? You ain't crying are you? Whatsa matter?'

'I don't know, Marrie.'

I closed my eyes, squeezing the tears down my face in black streaks, and leaned against the bars of the cage.

'Get off me you fucker.'

'Shut up or I'll belt you again.'

We arrived at the baths. Theoretically, this was a well-organized lesson, with the students divided into groups according to ability, and one teacher assigned to each group. In reality, it was never a lesson and always a disaster.

A screaming horde of adolescents tumbled from the coach and pelted through the swinging doors of the baths, plastering attendants against the walls and trampling underfoot any younger children who were unfortunate enough to be leaving at this time. They stormed on to the pool side and jumped in, disregarding instructions but careful to make as big a splash as possible. Whistles blew and voices shrilled.

'Into your groups. Groups. *Groups!*'

Instructors, retained by the council, refused to remain on the premises on Thursday afternoons.

Timmy pulled Lynda's swimming costume off and she burst into tearful hysterics. Gaylord didn't seem to realize that he must surface for air occasionally, and every few minutes one of the children hauled him up from the bottom. Highly chlorinated water makes Belinda ill and she vomited continually into the pool. Marrie had dashed into a cubicle, locked the door, and was now screeching over the top:

'You can all fuck off, I'm not going in that pissy old pool. Oh, look at Belinda!'

Shrill screams of laughter hammered at the skylights as she watched Belinda throw up. Several boys were holding a contest to determine who could splash the most water on me in a single dive-bomb. Philip won. Soaked to the skin with chlorine and vomit-tinged water I bellowed:

'Swim to the other side and back ten times, please. Yes that's right, but come back. Back. *Don't stay over there.*'

Abel had climbed out and was sleeping beside the pool while Alistair and Rob fought underwater. Greta and Kitty were comparing bosoms. I galloped around the pool and barked,

'Go back again. I didn't say stop. Ten times. Don't you understand?'

They swam to the opposite side and stopped, smiling and waving to me.

A prolonged blast of the whistle indicating the lesson's

end was, of course, ignored. Marrie ran from the cubicle and jumped in the pool shouting,

'You can all fuck off. I'm not getting out of this pool because I haven't had my swimming lesson.'

As the whistle blew for the fourth time two burly lifeguards dashed through the doorway and began pulling children from the water by the hair. This seemed to encourage the others to vacate the pool unassisted, and they all quickly disappeared into the cubicles.

Rob ran from his dressing-room, naked, and jumped into the pool, closely followed by a lifeguard. Peeping over the top of her cubicle, Marrie shrieked.

'Swim faster, Rob! Don't let the bastard get you. Kick him in the face.'

It was a brief skirmish. The guard, blood washing down from his bruised nose, towed Rob to the edge of the pool and sent him skidding into the dressing-room.

Gradually they dressed and appeared, crowding around the swing doors. Marrie and John rolled on the floor, pummelling and biting at one another while Brian smacked Jack on the head with a wet towel. Humiliated, Jack ran into the ladies' loo. Gaylord stood stiffly by the pool's edge, unbending legs jammed into their sockets, hands covering face, and growled,

'I want my beads.'

Suddenly he grasped the handle of a door marked 'Private' and tried to pull it off, while one of the lifeguards sprinted towards him. With Stewart in pursuit, Gaylord ran the length of the pool, seized one of the cubicle doors and wrenched it from its hinges. In uncontrollable fury he threw it at Stewart. It sank into fourteen feet of water, as Stewart pulled him towards the door.

'Now march out in orderly fashion and get into the coach. Quietly, please.'

Attendants and patrons locked themselves in the office as our students stampeded out, scratching and kicking at one another, screaming obscenities. In the rear, Stewart pulled a struggling Gaylord in the direction of the coach. A passing housewife strode towards Mabel and said,

'What school is this? I'm going to report you all. Look at that boy picking on the little coloured fellow. I don't think racial prejudice should be tolerated in our schools. This is . . .'

Stewart hit Gaylord's brown head with a clenched fist, and the little coloured fellow bit the kind lady on one tit. She screamed and fell against a tree as Gaylord was dragged into the coach.

We were half-way to the school, students happily flinging spitballs and chewing gum aimlessly about the coach, when Gaylord jumped up and tried to smash the window with his hands. Before Stewart and Brian could reach him he had ripped out one of the seats and thrown it against the windscreen. Brakes loudly protesting, the large vehicle bounced to a halt while Gaylord was once again flattened out in the aisle. Stewart and Brian assumed their former positions astride the prostrate figure and we continued on to school.

'How did swimming go?' He was carefully trimming the small, grey moustache.

'Bloody awful. It was a foul waste of time, as usual.'

Frozen, lidless eyes stared around the room. The hand-mirror smashed on to the table top as he snaked out of his armchair.

'Damn it, I don't know why you can't do it. *I* never have any trouble. I've shown you how to teach a swimming class before. One of you should be able to take the whole lot of them. You're just rotten teachers.'

I knew he could do it, and I knew we couldn't. Carve us a piece of fear from your 'Power Sceptre' and we'll try again. Gotta be hard in this game.

Faces assumed expressions of 'Hurt'. I dusted off my eyelashes and curled an eyeball around my cigarettes, too tired to light up.

'Ring the bloody bell and get everyone to class. They should all be working.'

CHAPTER SEVENTEEN

'HE'S back! Oi, Miss, dontcha wanna see him? He's back!'

'Who's back?'

'Ronnie Platt.'

'Very funny joke. Your sense of humour is sick.'

'S'truth. You don't believe nothin'. Come see.'

I went and saw him crawling on the hall floor searching for a place to hide his cigarettes. So they had sent him back from Borstal for one last chance. If he didn't behave now he would be sent down for the full three-year sentence.

'Hi, Ronnie. Welcome back.'

' 'Lo. Yeah. Better than that crap heap I was in.'

'You sure of that? You've only been back for five minutes. Anyway, it's nice to hear that we're a bit better than a Borstal. Where are you living?'

'Oh you know, a hostel. Some git in charge there and we have to call him Uncle.'

'Uncle what?'

'Just Uncle. What're you on about?'

Ronnie was sent to Borstal following his last truancy from school. It was absence that lasted for three months, and police had abandoned the search when he was accidentally discovered in an elegant suburb, shacked up with a very wealthy woman twenty-odd years older than he.

Larceny, pilfering, and absconding comprised his unspectacular police record, giving no indication of his basically vicious nature. He was the only boy in the school capable of remorseless murder, and the only one whose character was built on a foundation of cruelty.

Corruption of his personality was scarcely surprising. He had been weaned on violence. As a small child he had witnessed constant, searing arguments between his parents, during one of which his father had gouged out his mother's eye. Shortly after this incident, the father had vanished, leaving Mrs. Platt to support and raise Ronnie and three younger brothers.

Focusing all of her frustrations and rage on Ronnie, Mrs. Platt beat him mercilessly for real, suspected, and imaginary offences, using chains, tyre levers, belts or whatever was close to hand. One morning he had arrived at school unable to move from the waist up. Asking what was wrong, Seamus rested a hand on Ronnie's shoulder. The boy groaned and sweat poured down his face.

'It's me back, Sir.'

We were unable to inspect his back, as shirt and lacerated bits of flesh were glued together with congealed blood and mucus. The beating had been administered with a poker for a reason too trifling to recall.

We had tried to obtain an order placing him in 'Care and Protection', but the Children's Officer refused to act. Now that he had returned from Borstal it was seen fit to place him in care. For the past fifteen years he had marinated in a Violence Wine, turned occasionally with a bicycle chain, and removing him now would not obliterate that flavouring agent. He had been thoroughly soaked for too long. It was just too late. Contain, don't teach, and next year turn him loose.

'Like them earrings.'

'Thanks. Have your ears pierced and I'll give them to you for Christmas next.'

'Ya don't look very good. Yer looking real old, about twenty-five. Ya sick or somethin'?'

I should look twenty-five on my best days. The children

regarded age as a prize to be awarded according to popularity, not something to be judged realistically. The better they liked one, the younger that teacher was thought to be.

'I'm never sick and I never look good. I'm just tired.'

'Whatcha got them clothes on for?'

I was wearing my smart ensemble for this season: jeans, sweat shirt and sandals.

'I'm the art teacher now. I wear these every day.'

'Art teacher? Oi, I got you then?'

'That's right. You've got me. You've all got me.'

'Miss MacMichael. Miss MacMichael. Come to the office at once!'

The tannoy, having burped forth this summons, slid once again into silence. My class, busy shattering the few pieces of chalk which we had removed from the local quarry, visibly relaxed. Tension dissipated as each student felt the joy of temporary reprieve. None of them had been selected as the focal point of Seamus' current displeasure. They continued to sculpt with renewed vigour and, as hammers battered away at the soft blocks of stone, the chalk was rapidly transformed into fine white powder. Dust hung thick in the humid air of the shelter and blanketed every object with a gritty film. A few heads swivelled towards me.

'You're in for it now, Miss.'

'Whatcha done ta the old git today?'

'If that fucking old sod says anything, Miss, I ain't done it.'

'Will you *please* get on with your sculpting! *No*, Barrie, don't smash it with the hammer. Use the screwdriver to shape the stone and then smooth it with sandpaper. Oh God, no! Now you've broken it again. Can't you understand that we don't have any more chalk?'

Barrie's surly, diamond-shaped face turned towards me.

'Well you can always get some more, cantcha?'

'If you want to come and carry it for me I will. Right now you'll have to make do with what you have. Now get on with it until I come back.'

I ran from the shelter. My exit signalled the beginning of a thunderous uproar as students shrieked obscenities at one another and pounded viciously at the pieces of chalk. As I sped towards the office I could hear, fading mercifully into the distance, the sound of stones shattering on the shelter walls as my class abandoned themselves to an unsupervised chalk stone battle. The sound of Nick's transistor, turned on full volume, floated through the school as I reached the office door.

Seamus stood drumming his stringy fingers on the piano top. Mabel, clutching a sheaf of papers eagerly in her hands, was gazing raptly at the parchment face. She glanced in my direction as I rushed through the doorway and then turned back to Seamus. He continued to drum on the piano top and glared at me.

'You've got a problem.'

'I have?' I was plagued by an abundance of problems and speculated nervously upon which particular one was receiving Seamus' full attention.

'Ronnie Platt's mother just rang.'

I failed to see any connection between Mrs. Platt and my problems. Seamus was enraged by my lack of perception and left the piano. He slid around me in a circle, snarling hoarsely.

'Don't you know anything about these kids? You're supposed to know *all* about them. Christ! You can't teach and you don't bother to do your homework either. Just inefficient!'

He stopped in front of me and glared from under drooping, half-closed eyelids.

'God! How can I run my school with a staff like this? It's your business to know that Ronnie's mother baths him once a week.'

'She what?'

'She baths him. Like a baby. Washes him, rinses him, and dries him off. Like a baby.'

'But Seamus, he's seventeen.'

'Don't tell me how old my students are! Why don't you know about him?'

'This wasn't in his file. I read it.'

'You're supposed to know it anyway. Mabel did.'

She beamed, fanning herself slightly with the fistful of papers. Seamus paused in front of the mirror to inspect his image. He raised and lowered his eyebrows, smoothed down his tie and opened his mouth. Leaning close to the mirror he stuck out his tongue and examined it minutely for flaws and discolorations. Satisfied, he snapped his mouth closed, gave a final pat to his jacket and slithered back to the centre of the room, craning his neck to catch one last glimpse of his impeccable reflection. I waited.

Crossing to his desk, Seamus opened a drawer and took out his gold-backed buffer. He began to polish his glistening nails.

'This morning Mrs. Platt rang and said she had discovered an ugly sore on Ronnie's . . . uh, um, on Ronnie's er, private parts while she was bathing him. She said she thought we should know about it.'

He slammed the buffer down on the desk and glowered at me.

'This information should have come from you, not Mrs. Platt.'

I gawked.

'Seamus, I don't bath Ronnie, I just teach him. For one hour a day.'

'Don't give me that crap. You don't teach him or anyone else. Your job is to keep your ears open. Hear things from the kids and report them to me. You could have heard about this if you'd kept your ears open.'

'Seamus, I don't think it's something that Ronnie would discuss.'

'That dirty-minded little bastard? He's probably *shown*

it to half the school! It sounds like VD to me and I wouldn't be surprised if he's passed it on to everyone else here. Mabel has very kindly volunteered to drive Ronnie to the clinic today. He paused and nodded his gratitude to Mabel. She fanned rapidly at her sweating face and beamed. Seamus raised his voice to a bellow. 'We'd better all hope to God that Ronnie hasn't got the pox! Now get back to class and *listen*! If you can't teach, at least you can get some information out of these kids occasionally!'

'Sir!'

I pivoted and rushed back to the shelter. It was a shambles. Broken stones, overturned water buckets, and smashed ceramics littered the cement floor. Wet clay had been smeared liberally all over the shelter walls in wet, red streaks. Shredded newspaper, soaked in glue and intended for papier mâché constructions, had been plastered decoratively on to the chair and table legs. Most of the caretaker's tools were missing while the remainder lay broken and strewn over the table tops. All removable portions of the kiln had been removed. My class, oblivious of the destruction in the shelter, were clustered in a sociable group, shrieking at one another over the din of the transistor radio.

I sighed and leaned against a damp, clay-streaked wall. Timmy, suddenly aware of my presence, turned and shouted.

'Oi, she's back! What's Sir want, Miss?'

I turned off the transistor and sloshed through the water to the gleeful students.

'I told you to get on with your work, not destroy the classroom.'

'This hole ain't no classroom, Miss. Any other school has rooms, not fucking air-raid shelters.'

'Don't interrupt! I want this mess cleaned up in one half-hour. I want the tools located and I want the parts of that kiln found and put back in place. This chalk was the last equipment of any kind for art, and until I am able to

find more you may bring your academic work to the shelter and do it during craft hour. Now get busy.'

They moaned, cursed, and hissed at one another. They got to work and cleaned up the shelter.

Ronnie's test was positive. He had contracted syphilis, and the staff convened in shocked, hushed silence. Seamus, purple hued, pranced in the centre of his office.

'My school. *My school!* Do you know what will happen if we have an epidemic here? *In my school!* Mabel and I are going to talk to all these slags and find out just who's been having it off with whom; if any of you discuss the subject outside this room I will crucify you. All of you. Now get back to your classes and when I call your students out you send them running.'

We fled back to our respective classrooms. For the next three days classes were continually interrupted as students were summoned by the belching tannoy. They sauntered to the office and slunk back, shamefaced. Staff averted eyes, the students chuckled and invented jokes. We all waited.

On the third day we once again gathered in Seamus' office to hear results of the mass interviews. Apparently, most of the students had slept, at one time or another, with the rest of the student body. The children had been a bit vague regarding times and places, but it was obvious that none had been discriminatory about partners. Seamus quivered in rage and the school quaked in fear.

'They all have to have blood tests. We can't let these slags leave school with the bloody pox! Spread it all over England in the next week. Jesus! If there were any control around here this wouldn't happen.' He danced and skittered, twisting his gold ring around his right little finger.

'Mabel!' She jumped to attention and waddled, smiling to Seamus' side, 'Send out the usual permission slips for the parents to sign but for God's sake don't tell them why we're making the tests. These parents will sign. Most of them can't read anyway but they're like sheep. Can't bloody read but they can sign their names. Should see them down at the Labour. Conor! Are you listening?'

I started and turned my eyes from the sight of Gaylord. He had climbed to the top of a tall tree just outside the window and was hanging by his knees from a very fragile branch. The tree bent and swayed under the boy's weight. Oblivious to the danger and, apparently, to the shrieks of Marrie on the ground below, Gaylord swung contentedly upside down.

'Yes, Sir.'

He pivoted, patting his white linen suit into place and noticed a streak of grey dirt on the trousers. He flicked and dusted at the mark. Discussion was forgotten as he searched for the clothes-brush and viciously attacked the white cloth. We watched, silently, until he abandoned the attempt to remove the offensive smudge. Straightening, he smashed the clothes-brush on to the piano top and glared at the staff.

'That's what I mean about animals. Can't keep clean at home and it's like a pigsty here. When we finish I want all classes suspended while we clean this school. And I want it *clean*! We'll stay here until midnight if that's what it takes.'

He paused dramatically, involuntarily picking at the grey streak of dirt. His opaque eyes crackled with rage as he stepped forward towards the staff.

'Now! If any parents do happen to be literate enough to read and intelligent enough to ask about these tests they just might ring the school. I doubt it but it may happen. You're to tell them that we suspect a minor infection has been contracted and we're making sure that none of their bloody offspring is diseased. And one word about VD to anyone, parents, school authorities, any other teachers . . . *one word* and I'll have you out of my school in five minutes. Now get back to your classes and tell those pigs to clean up the school.'

The clinic nurse arrived and took blood samples. The girls screamed and fainted, while the boys proved their manhood by stoically braving the needle. Literate parents rang the school and were reassured. Seamus remained closeted in his office, presumably planning his strategy in the event of an epidemic.

The test results arrived in a sealed hand-delivered envelope. Negative. Ronnie was the only pox-afflicted member of St. Steven's. Seamus relaxed and buffed his shining nails. Mabel stretched her mouth into a wide grimace and noted down Ronnie's clinic appointments. No one mentioned the episode. Neither children nor parents were aware of the nature of the blood tests and my tentative suggestion, to Seamus, that the students should be given a lecture on venereal disease was met with derision.

'Bloody stupid idea. They don't have it, Conor, and I can't have classes here in sex and VD without explaining it to the parents. How am I going to tell that to the parents? Uh?'

'Seamus, it's better that they know about it than for them to have it. Most of these kids don't even know what it is, and they're still having it off with anyone at any opportunity.'

'That's not my problem. Out of school they can do what they want. As long as there's nothing wrong in *my* school they can do what they want outside.'

I went back to the shelter. Timmy stopped demolishing a table and turned to me.

'Oi, Miss, them tests. Me old girl still wants to know what they was.'

'Nothing, Timmy. Just testing for an unimportant blood infection. You don't have it, so let's get to work.'

We worked.

CHAPTER EIGHTEEN

I KNOCKED on the office door. Although there was no reply I could hear him picking out notes on the piano. I knocked again, opened the door and walked in.

Seamus was coiled around two 'G' sharps on the grand piano which, in carved and polished splendour, nearly filled the small room. It was the first time I had ever seen him in shirtsleeves. Jacket and waistcoat now lay neatly folded over the back of an armchair. Pencils, papers, and pens were meticulously arranged on the music stand. A sheet of music floated to the carpet as he swivelled to stare at me.

'Get out. Can't you see I'm bloody well composing? Always something. Damn it, what do you want?' A twine fist crushed middle 'C'.

'We're almost out of clay, Seamus. The kids like pottery, and it's almost the only craft they all will stick at. Couldn't we order some more clay, please?'

'Of course we can't order more. You seem to think we can just run out and buy whatever we like. Always someone wanting something.'

'Seamus, we don't have any materials at all for art or craft, and I just can't afford to buy any more out of my own pocket. We're out of paint, out of lino . . .'

'Go and ask builder supply shops to give us some. If you weren't so damned lazy and went to some of these people, they'd be glad to donate offcuts.'

'I've asked and they aren't giving. Come on, just a hundredweight more will last to the end of term, if Gaylord will stop making those huge monstrosities. He's used more clay than all the rest put together.'

'No, we won't order more, but we'll make our own. Yes. That's what we'll do. Make our own.'

Composing was forgotten. Zinc yellow wrinkles creased

the scaly parchment around his mouth as his lips parted to reveal brown fangs. Fissures cracked around the lidless eyes that glittered grey reflections of the music notes. He sidled over to his jacket.

'Yes, yes. Make our own clay.'

He fumbled in a desk drawer for his silver-handled clothes-brush and began languidly to brush invisible dust from the folded garments.

I gaped.

'Make clay? Seamus, do you know how long that takes? Where are we going to get raw clay, anyway?'

'Where? Why this soil is all pure clay once you dig down two feet. We're built on clay here.' We are indeed. 'I want to deepen the pond in the animal pen and cement it anyway, so we'll start out there. Once we dig the clay out we'll get some oil drums, put it in there and wash it down. Make our own clay. Yes. We do everything here.'

My hearing must be impaired. It was normal once, just like my sight, my mind, my nerves, and my life.

'The animal pen?'

'You must be willing to do anything when you teach at St. Steven's. If you aren't, this isn't the place for you and you can get out. I can run this school on my own. Piece of cake.'

Soggy angel cake and rock buns.

'Seamus, it will take months to wash and sieve that clay. It has to settle several times and all the impurities must be removed. I need clay *now*.'

'Now you don't, and don't tell *me* how to make clay. I've done it hundreds of times. From now on you and your classes will spend the craft hour digging in the animal pen. Who do you have with you now?'

'Mabel's class.'

'Good. Good. All fine workers.' He switched on the tannoy and barked into the speaker.

'In future will Miss MacMichael's classes report to her at the animal pen, wearing Wellington boots and overalls.

There will be no craft classes until we have completed some outdoor tasks. Mabel's class will report there immediately, ready to work.'

He turned to me.

'Now I want you to dig down at least four feet into the pond. Have the boys get the wheelbarrows and dump each load by the fence in the woods.'

'I thought you said we'd use oil drums.'

'We don't *have* any drums. For now we'll just make a large pile on the ground and see about shifting it later.'

My eyelashes curved around tennis-ball orbs. I blinked.

'Well, don't stand. Move. And don't come back in here again. I'm composing and I will not be disturbed for anything or anyone.'

He hung the jacket and waistcoat over the back of the armchair again and sat down at the piano, glowering at some notes on his paper.

I wandered out of the back door towards the animals, was struck down by an aggressive May sunbeam, and spun back inside the school. I put on my blue-lensed glasses, bikini and white Wellington boots, and kicked my way through tangled ultra-violet rays. Bloated plastic figurines lined up at the windows to watch my progress across the lawn.

Stewart lounged against the wire gate to the pen. Sullen and resentful, the others squatted or sat on the pavement before him.

'What's it gonna be now, Miss?'

'We are going to dig clay from the pond and wash it down to use in craft. Sir's orders.'

'Dig that shit?'

'Fucking hell, Miss, look at it!'

'Look at it! Smell it! You think I'm makin' any fucking ashtray out of that you can get stuffed.'

Barbara the goose, several ducks, and an array of egg-laying chickens were penned in the area. In the centre was a shallow, drainless pond which, during the rains, spilled over with water. The past few weeks had been dry, and most moisture had evaporated, leaving a thick mud consisting of urine and excrement. The smell was overwhelming.

'Jeeeeeeeeeeeesus H. Christ. Those fucking animals drink that crap.'

'I ain't digging in no shit. Whose fucking idea was this?'

'Boss Man the lady said, you git.'

'Well he can get stuffed.'

'Now look. I'm not exactly looking forward to this either, but it has to be done and I won't do it all by myself. You boys stop moaning and go get some shovels and spades. Oh yes, and the two wheelbarrows. We have to do it, so we may as well get busy.'

Grumbling, they turned towards the tool shed. Mabel rounded the corner, a smile pasted on her thick mouth.

'I saw you coming out here.'

'Um.'

'I imagine Seamus will have complaints from the neighbours.' She beamed.

'Why? Don't they approve of children digging up animal shit?'

The smile fluttered away to perch on a sunbeam, then drifted towards the chicken coop. Mabel raced after it, captured the elusive Expression and pasted it firmly in place. She tugged at a strand of greasy hair.

'It's your bikini.'

'What about it? I'm not indecently exposed. I have on my chic white Wellingtons.'

She held the smile in place, preventing its escape.

'But the neighbours.'

'Mabel, what *about* the neighbours?'

'Uh, well, you see, they pay your salary, you know, and they have a right to object to your attire. It's really not very dignified.'

'My *salary*? You tell any cackling old cow that rings

up that I'll put my clothes on when she raises my wage. If I have to shovel shit and listen to "eff off" all day I'll do it in the nude if I like.'

'Oh *I'm* not objecting. No, no. I just thought I'd tell you.'

'Thanks.'

The smile tumbled down on to an egg nestling in the weeds. She picked it up and began backing around the corner of the building, only to rocket forward and sprawl on the pavement, mowed down by Ronnie's wheelbarrow as he sped towards the pen.

'Oh sorry. I didn't bleeding well see ya, did I?'

She crawled towards the school, smile in hand.

'Hurry up, for God's sake. Come on, Ronnie, you and Timmy take the barrows when they're full and dump them by the fence. Not all along the fence. Make a pile. The rest of us will dig.'

'I'm not fucking well going to do no digging.'

'I don't see that pissy old bastard out here.'

'He doesn't have to be. He's the Head.'

'Bollocks to this school. I thought we were here to learn things.'

'I find this very educational. Come on, grab a spade. Here, give me that.'

Shovel in hand, I opened the gate and led the expedition to the side of the pond. God, what a stink! I jumped in, sinking to the knees in fetid goat dung and urine, clumps of which slid slowly down the inside of my boots. An army of rainbow-hued flies rose angrily from the slime and buzzed in a wide circle, coming to rest on my bikini top.

'Oi, Miss, you've got those igy flies all over you.'

'Oi, whatsa difference between that thing you got on and a bra?'

'Not much. but I trust that you can't see through this.'

Motionless children ringed the pond, watching as I sank inextricably into the animal dung.

'Please come on and get busy.'

Frieda and Stewart jumped in, splattering my midriff with goat and chicken shit.

'I'll start here, you work over there. And dig deep.'

Immune to the stench, I settled to the task, hopeful that my industrious example would spur the class into action.

'Look out where you're throwing it.'

Stewart aimed for the barrow, missed, and a muddy load of goat droppings hit Frieda in the back.

'You stupid bastard.'

She threw a shovelful of shit at Timmy, hitting him on the arm, and ducked as he tossed back a particularly offensive pile of green and ochre animal crap. It smacked against my head and I stood up, excrement dripping down my back and over my bikini.

Ronnie and Timmy sat on the chicken coop, bent double with rude laughter.

'Look at shitty old Miss.'

'Oooh! Phew! Don't she just stink!'

'Look. I've had enough. Take those damned barrows and empty them now or you can come down here and dig while I recline on the lovely coop.'

They pushed off with the barrows.

'Oi, Miss, I think I've found clay.'

'Stew, that's a rock. We aren't to the clay yet.'

'He can go fuck himself if he thinks I'm going to use this in craft.'

'Oi, Miss, is this clay?'

'No, Louise, it's hardened excrement.'

'What's excrement?'

'Faeces. Shit. Crap. The stuff I'm standing in, covered with, and digging.'

'Oh.'

I dropped my shovel into the muck and it sank out of sight. As I bent to retrieve it, one of the ducks flew on to my back and began to peck at my dung-covered neck, squawking in fury as I rolled it into the pond. I began digging again, my hands slipping on the slimy handle.

'How long do we have to go on? We're anyway three feet down now.'

'Till I tell you to stop.'

The bell rang. Sun had dried the excrement in which I was coated and it flaked from my hair and crackled on my arms and back. I wiped my forehead and left a streak of tan shit.

Combing his hair, Seamus appeared on the outside of the fencing. He pulled out a silk handkerchief and delicately covered his nostrils.

'Fine. Fine. You're doing a great job. At this rate we'll be able to cement the pond this week.'

Brown statues, modelled in dry excrement stared at the immaculate figure with sun-stroked eyes.

'Are we cementing the pond or getting clay for craft?'

'Oh, you know.' He vaguely fanned the air with his free hand. 'Both. Yes, yes. Both. Miss MacMichael, you carry on. The rest of you, go take a shower and then get back to your classroom.'

Resting my shovel in a pile of goat dung I waited for my next crew of shit-shovellers. All I wanted was some clay.

CHAPTER NINETEEN

BELINDA shuffled into the air-raid shelter and sat down, watching me fish sponges from a bucket of dirty water. The kiln was turned on to 'high'. Pink sweat drizzled from the pores of the brick walls, dampening the chill, chalk-coated cement floor. Light from the neon stick ran in rivulets through heavy, humid air, forcing its way through sticky clay that hung, suspended in wet layers.

I had sent my class, coughing and sweating, out of the air-raid shelter. Most of them had taken sculpture or clay and returned to the Home Room, but Jeff and Roy, both congenitally ill, had elected to stay and throw pots on the wheel. Jeff suffered brain dehydration and softening of the bones, was slightly palsied, and became dangerously ill several times during each school year. I begged him to leave the room. Wizened and shaking, he refused.

'I wanna make my Mum a flower bowl, don't I, Miss? How'm I gonna take the wheel outside?'

'You can't. It weighs over two hundred pounds. Do something else today.'

'It's like this here every day. I'm good at pottery and I don't want to do nothing else.'

Torpid tears rattled in my brain. He was one of the few children who was really skilful in pottery and it was his sole talent. Totally illiterate, unable to solve the simplest problems in addition, and physically unfit for PT in any form, he was ecstatic when he discovered an ability to create beautiful pots. So he stayed. He will probably be sick for the next four weeks.

'My Mother died last Saturday.'

I dropped a sponge.

'What, Belinda?'

'Mum died.'

Her mother had been bed-ridden with ulcers for almost a year and had refused to be nursed by anyone other than Belinda and her sister Frieda. The girls, hardened by life when they were very young, often arrived at school vividly describing bits of intestine and cellular matter that they had discovered when attending to their mother. They reeked of rotting muscle and the stench of putrefied bones penetrated their clothes, hair, and skin. Every morning they showered and changed at school, and still the odour clung to their nails; it oozed from pores and unwashed eyeballs.

'Know what I was doing when she died?'

'No.'

'Eating egg and chips.'

Merciful Mary!

'When was the funeral, Belinda?'

'Oh, I dunno. It was a coupla days ago I guess. We didn't go because Dad said it cost a pound.'

'I'm really very sorry, Belinda. Are you looking after your Dad now?'

My stomach curled at the thought.

'Yeah. Me'nd Frieda. We can't always find him, but he's usually hanging around the same pubs.'

Although Belinda's mother and 'dad' had cohabited at intervals over the past twenty years, he was the actual father of neither girl. Belinda's mother, a prostitute, had borne eight children and had given the four eldest away. Home, for the girls, meant searing arguments between mother and 'dad', separations and reconciliations. And a throng of anonymous men brought home by mother. Eight years ago the girls were locked out of the house and taken into care, being placed in a home. 'Dad' paid occasional visits, but their mother vanished completely, an event that profoundly affected Belinda. She became inhibited and depressed, unable to concentrate and a bully when in the company of her peers. She was incapable of making the slightest decision and unable to work or amuse herself alone. She demanded the complete attention of anyone in attendance, yet did not appear to respond positively to excessive amounts of care and solicitude. Gradually these symptoms abated as she became reconciled to the fact that her mother would not return.

Both girls were placed in a foster home in the country where they appeared to be happy and began to regain self-confidence. As soon as they had begun to settle, some five years ago, their mother and 'dad' reappeared, announced that they had been married and wanted the girls back. The case was disputed but, as no legal adoption had taken place, Belinda and Frieda were eventually sent back to the natural mother.

A few months ago the girls' younger brother Peter had

been sent to St. Steven's with a background of playing truant, larceny, and arson. Like his sisters, Peter had spent most of his life in foster homes, but was reunited with his mother, two sisters, and brother about a year ago.

The mother had retired from her profession, but 'dad' was now grooming the girls for careers as prostitutes, and selected various, rather elderly, men with whom they regularly slept. We had tried to obtain an order placing the sisters in care once again, but no one would take responsibility. The Children's Officer kicked the leather-encased problem to the Education Department, who tossed it back to the Welfare Department. They, in turn, batted it to the Health Department, who threw it back to the Children's Officer. Meantime, the girls were learning a lucrative trade and Frieda would be sixteen in the summer. Everyone could grin in relief and resume the ball-game until Belinda reached school-leaving age.

'I'd like to go and live with my Nan but she can't keep us.'

Doesn't want to, you mean.

'Never mind, come by for a cup of tea on Saturday if you're around the Common. It's easier to talk there.'

'Yeah. Ta Miss.'

At eight o'clock on Saturday morning my maladjusted doorbell rang. It took a perverse pleasure in chiming at three in the morning and eight on Saturday. I grovelled on the floor for my lenses and eyelashes, hunted in my drawer for some peace and quiet, failed to find anything and sailed to the door on a raft made of transparent wishes. It was Belinda.

'You sure look bad without your make-up, Miss.'

'It's all right. You have to look at me, I don't. What on earth are you doing here at this hour?'

'Dad drove us in. He's got some business.'

Uncharitable thoughts flooded my befogged brain.

'Well, come in and make us some tea while I get dressed.'

'Put on your make-up first. You look just awful.'

The joys of a lazy Saturday morning.

Belinda tagged after me while I shopped, helped me cook lunch and washed up afterwards. Apparently she had nothing to do, and was content to spend her time regaling me with tales of horror from her childhood. She regarded her background as commonplace, and discussed events of her past without a trace of bitterness. I felt quite ill. A disturbed nerve tapped out my rules of life on a swollen ear drum; I counted ladders in my stockings, smiled, and listened.

At three Frieda arrived with her boyfriend, a very drunk, twenty-seven-year-old barman.

'Tell Belinda she's got to come now. We have to go and find Dad.'

'Right now?'

'Yeah. The pubs are closing, aren't they? If we don't find him now we'll have to walk home won't we?'

They hurried down the stairs in search of 'dad' doing business in the pub. That night Frieda ran away with her boyfriend. Peter was picked up by the police on a larceny charge the following day.

Perturbed expressions were glued to balloon faces on Monday. They're here, they're gone, contain, don't teach. They'll all be sixteen someday.

CHAPTER TWENTY

I PULLED myself up the three flights of stairs by the iron railing. Seamus says there is no reason for us to be tired at the end of a day, so I'm tired for no reason. I missed a step and fell, ripping the knee from my stocking. Damn, I'm getting old. Elderly. Ancient. Past it.

'Oi, Miss.'

No, please God, no. I want peace and quiet. Rest in a health farm, with someone to feed me lemon juice and curl all three pairs of false eyelashes.

Marrie and her class-mate Patty were hanging over the railing outside my door, hair dangling down into the stairwell as they watched my faltering advance.

'Oi, there, hurry up old lady. We brung you sunthin'.'

Marrie's shriek thundered down the tubular vacuum, bounced back up and slapped me on the ear, then fell down the spiral stairs. A hundred shouting Marries reverberated up and down the ageing staircase.

'Marrie, do be a little more quiet. My head hurts.' I reached the top of the stairs and flopped against the coal-shed door. 'What do you have?'

'This here.' Marrie thrust a round, prickly mass at my abdomen. The grey thorns moved slightly and a black snout with quivering nostrils appeared. Thousands of fleas, dislodged by the change of position, scattered from the thorny mound and settled on Patty's silver cocktail dress which she was wearing, inexplicably, with her plimsolls. Dissatisfied, they moved, *en masse* to my arms, took a few ravenous bites, and returned home. I inched away.

'A hedgehog! How lovely. That's very thoughtful, girls, but I really have no place to keep a hedgehog here.'

'Oh, he ain't for you to keep, Miss. We caught him running down the Common so's to take to school with the other animals, but there ain't nobody there now. We're going to leave him here tonight'n' you bring him in the morning.'

I unlocked my door and they followed me in, Marrie still clutching the hedgehog and his parasites.

'Oh ain't this smart. Real posh. Ain't nothin' like a carpet for class, is it?' She put the animal and its friends down on my new carpet.

'Not on the carpet, Marrie, please. Honestly, I don't know what I'll do with him, even for tonight.'

'How about putting him in your bed? He'll like it there.'

'No! I mean, no, I don't think so. The kitchen's out because he'll crawl into that hole and fall between the walls. I just haven't a place.'

'The bathroom, Miss,' she shrieked, squashing the prickles to her bosom and dashing for the door. 'O.K. in here, Miss? It's only till the morning.'

'Oh sure, sure. Just what do I use to carry him to school? I'm certainly not going to ride buses through town holding a hedgehog in my arms.'

'Dontcha like him?' her face trembled, and the blue eyes watered. 'Here, pet him.'

'Oh, I like him, Marrie, he's beautiful. I just want a box or carrier.'

'Use that bag you carry all those fucking books in. He'll fit. We gotta go now. Ta, Miss. See ya.'

The front door slammed, leaving hedgehog and me alone together. Marrie had slung him on the bathroom floor and, after the first stunned moments, he began racing from one end of the tiny room to the other, sniffing and scratching, I closed the door and firmly resisted any temptation to bath, wash, or clean my teeth that evening. Thank God the loo wasn't in there. I shuddered. The kids love all animals and treat them with a kindness that they never bestow upon other human beings. The hedgehog scratched at the door. I went to bed, longing for a bath.

Next morning, bag in hand, I edged the bathroom door open and cautiously looked around the room. No hedgehog and no fleas. I stepped in and called out,

'Here, hedgehog.'

No hedgehog. No movement of any kind. Where in hell could he have gone? There were no hiding places, the window was shut . . . I stared at England's oldest bathtub, of which I was the reluctant owner. The artistic designer had seen fit to festoon the wall behind this rusting article with countless pipes of varying shape and size, and had left a small space between wall and tub to accommodate the three-dimensional mural. Although the crevice was small, it would certainly permit entry of a hedgehog. And his friends. I crawled over and lit a match. Black. Nothing. Hell, I grabbed an empty bag and ran for the bus.

'Where is he then?' Marrie screamed.

'Under my bath tub.'

'Stone me, Miss. Why'ud you let him get in there? I told you I should'a put him in your bed.'

'Yes, well come help me get him out after school.'

'I can't. Gotta go out, don't I?'

'Marrie, you brought him to me in the first place. I don't know anything about animals, and I've never even seen a hedgehog before.'

'I'll come tomorrow.'

After school I took a torch and looked into the crevice. The only object in sight was one peeling end of the tub. Assuming that he was at least a semi-vegetarian, I left some lettuce leaves on the floor, and thinking that he might be attracted by light, left the torch shining into the cavity. In the morning I learned that hedgehogs are neither attracted to lettuce nor light. Attempting to frighten him from his hiding place I got into the tub and jumped violently up and down on my stiletto heels, stopping only when I heard menacing cracks in the enamel. I got out of the tub and filled it with hot water, in case he was repelled by heat.

'Here, hedgehog, please come out. Here boy.'

I was late, earning leers from the plastic faces and a wrathful bellow from Seamus.

'This isn't a holiday camp, you know!'

'Yes, I know.'

'Marrie, are you coming round tonight to help me?'

'Can't, can I? Anyway, you fucking well lost our present to the school.'

'I haven't lost him, unfortunately. I know where he is

but I can't get him out. He hasn't eaten for two days and I'm afraid he'll die and begin to smell.'

Marrie screeched with delight at the prospect.

Patty suggested:

'Maybe he's hibernating.'

'They don't hibernate in the spring, Patty.'

An officious little tea-lady-cum-welfare assistant, soured by years in the institution, bustled past, glowering,

'Tea's up, ducks.'

That night, armed with two screwdrivers, I attacked the façade of the tub. The screws, rusty and rotten, refused to budge. I broke a screwdriver and began to pry at the piece of decayed wood with a chisel and claw hammer, finally ripping it from the tub. I squinted around the edges of the mouldy tub and saw him in the far corner. I pulled a towel from the rail and crawled around the end of the tub, tensed, ready to pounce and wrap the infected animal in my best towel. He scampered between the tub and far wall. I prodded him with the chisel and he wedged firmly, unable to move in any direction. I lay on the floor and pondered ways and means of rescuing a hedgehog. The only solution was to move the tub out from the wall. What a holiday camp.

I turned off the water supply to the flat, found a spanner and wrench, and began disconnecting the maze of pipes on the wall. At four in the morning I moved the tub out a few inches, threw the towel over the inert animal, and scooped him off the floor. Fleas and lice struggled to escape from the thick terry-cloth prison as I zipped him into my bag. I unzipped the bag and took him out again after deciding, regretfully, that he would smother. I wandered to the kitchen, diseased parcel in hand, selected my metal bread tin, and deposited the packet inside. Using the chisel I uncovered his wet snout, banged the lid of the container and placed it in the bath tub.

I removed my dignity, repairing the shreds, cleaned my false eyelashes and lay down on a holiday camp mattress.

Wild scratching and metallic clanging noises issued from the bathroom. I sat up in a maladjusted bed and listened, as the frantic clawing and sharp rolling increased in frenzy. Wrapping up in a bloodshot retina I floated to the bathroom, opened the door and gazed at the tub. The disease had climbed from my tin, overturned it, and was now scrambling from one end of the tub to the other, pushing the lid and container with him. I found a piece of string, replaced hedgehog in the tin and tied the lid down. As I closed the door, the tin lid began to thump up and down with monotonous regularity, as the animal sought to escape. Thc thumping continued throughout the night, accompanied my breakfast, and caused fellow commuters to leave the bus stop and travel on foot. I carried the thudding bread tin into the Hall.

'Whatcha got there, Miss?'

Marrie screamed, 'Is that my hedgehog? Fucking hell, you'll smother him.' Ripping frantically at the string, she freed the spiky animal and sped down the corridor to my classroom, temporary home of the school cat, clutching him against one hip. As she placed him on the floor, the cat arched, spat, and sprang. Hedgehog scampered to the wall, cat in pursuit, as she tried to bite the wet black nose. Fleas and lice changed homes.

Throughout the day the battle raged, cheered on by my class of spectators. Lessons were ignored.

'Come on, bite him.'

'Fuck it, stick her in the paw.'

'Shit, you got her!'

'Git him back! Scratch his bleeding eyes out!'

'Run. Run!'

'... he's under the sink.'

'... look out, here he comes ...'

'Oh you bastard! You poked her in the bleeding gut.'

Seamus opened the door and stared at combatants and shrieking onlookers. He stepped into the arena.

'What is this?'

'We brung a hedgehog. Miss brung him for us, didn't she?'

He glowered at me in fury as the cat ran over and sharpened her claws on his silk trouser leg.

'He certainly can't stay here. This is a classroom. Take him to the woods.' He kicked the cat across the room, where she lay mewing. The hedgehog ran up and perforated one ear.

'Fuck that! He got the bleeding cat!'

'Stone me! Get up you stupid sod and fight.'

'Shut up! Take this animal to the woods at once.'

Seamus saw a flea approaching and slammed the door behind him.

'Jeeesus, Miss, he *came* from the woods.'

'Old Seamus can just fuck off.'

'Take him back, as you were told.'

'I'll take him.'

'No, I will. I'm going to hide him, ain't I?'

The class and hedgehog disappeared into the woods, while I phoned a plumber to rebuild my bathroom.

The children's rapport with animals was one that they could never achieve with fellow human beings. They extended love, sympathy, and kindness, and the animals responded. Their hedgehog, ugly, infested, thorny, was found in the wood and taken home where he wrecked my room, exhausted my temper and split my nerves, only to be tossed back into the wood, unchanged in any way. They'll all be sixteen soon and be thrown back into the wood.

Marrie peeped in.

'Ta anyway, Miss. You take real good care of animals. Next time we find sunthin' we'll bring him to you again.'

Just one big holiday camp. Come feed the asses with your marshmallow knuckleduster.

CHAPTER TWENTY-ONE

It was going to be a bad day. Seamus had arrived late, enraged over a scratch on his Mercedes. When he entered in such a mood the entire school quaked in fearful expectancy. His wrath would focus on a minor incident in the Staff Room, or centre on a troublesome child. On those rare days when sanity prevailed and no scapegoat was readily available, Seamus would uproot past difficulties, probing cankers with a fork of molten fear and scalding disturbed brains with a vat of simmering sarcasm.

Assembly progressed in an orderly fashion, the children withdrawn and waiting, the staff flattened against walls with worried expressions. Mabel left the room to summon Seamus for his post-assembly lecture and the silence danced from the tannoy, beating against crumbling walls and thumping on sagging window frames with a raucous, sickening beat. It coated the eyeballs, gummed the throat, dizzied nerve endings, squeezing and compressing us into solid sticks of cartilage.

Leaning on his shapeless cane of fear, Seamus carved a passage through the solidified silence and slithered to the front of the room. The children were magnetized by non-existent patterns on the worn floor. The staff stared at the children. Seamus glared at each of us in turn, and buffed his silver nails.

'I'll give you one chance. Will the boy or girl who stole Mrs. Riding's apples step forward at once. I will not have neighbours complaining that students from my school have been stealing fruit from their gardens.'

'Desmond, you're a fruit. Step forward, ya old moo.'

'Shut up, Marrie! Well?'

No one moved and the silence crammed up one's nostrils with slimy tentacles, and blocked the intestines. The children were still intently studying lines on the floor. I turned and gazed from the window. Red and orange blades of grass sprang from festering classroom foundations, and a pool of pus bubbled in the animal pen. Trees in the wood sprouted rancid appendages in place of branches, which whipped and tore at their own roots. I turned back to the Hall.

Seamus slammed his manicure set on to a table and his stringy limbs began to shake, as his face changed, in colour, from crimson to ashen and settled into deep puce.

'Is no one going to admit to this crime?'

No one moved.

'Right! Form a double line at the door and we will march over to Mrs. Riding's house so that she can identify the guilty party. I promise you that I will crucify that boy or girl when she makes the identification. Does anyone have a change of mind? No? All right, line up.'

Silently, still fascinated by the appearance of the scarred floor, they formed a queue by the door.

'Right.'

Bony, dressed in linen, silk and rage, the wraith-like figure snaked out of the front door, followed by a subdued student body.

Silence rolled back into the Hall, through the windows, under the door, through the chunks of sagging plaster, in a thick, choking fog. It settled on the tables, covered the windowsills and piled up on the floor in swelling drifts of mucilage. I hung one ear drum on the pegboard and waited.

The front door opened and the double file of students marched back into the Hall, still enchanted by the splintered wooden floor. Seamus rattled to the front of the room, scourging the turbid silence with his pronged wand of fear. Lidless eyes speared each suffering child, as his rusty voice shocked the stillness into agonized waves of slippery retreat.

'It seems that we're back to square one. Mrs. Riding

saw only the hands of the culprit over the top of her fence, and it's rather difficult to identify a thief from a pair of hands.'

An unctuous smile cracked the yellow tissue-paper cheeks and flaked scale from the matted eyeballs. He traced a fissure in the eye socket with one pointed fingernail.

'I have, however, discovered an interesting fact about these apples. Mrs. Riding tells me that they are extremely poisonous when green, and these apples are not yet ripe. The child who stole those apples will be ill for days.'

The smile had broadened, splitting dried epidermis into crinkled sections. Seamus smoothed back his wavy hair and prodded cellophane wads with colourless reptilian eyes.

In the front row, Philip began to sway, and he fixed Seamus with a cross-eyed stare.

'Oi, that ain't true, is it?'

'Of course. I just told you.'

'Oi, Sir, I took them apples, but I ain't gonna be real sick. I don't feel sick.'

The smile glittered beneath malevolent eyes.

'You *will* be sick. Those apples will swell up and burst your belly, Philip. You'll do yourself an injury with this stealing.'

Philip's hand explored his stomach while his face turned olive green. He rushed from the Hall and Seamus' delighted voice pursued him down the corridor.

'Go see Mrs. Greely and she'll do what she can to see you survive.'

I had clashed with Philip a few weeks earlier when he first entered St. Steven's. Tiny, tough, with a face like a decadent prune, he spent his school days bullying the weaker children. Swaggering, snarling, spitting, he refused to work, informing each teacher in his charming manner,

'I ain't gonna do nothin'.'

'Get your notebook and pencil and come do some handwriting for me.' I was pursuing him around the back lawn during a morning craft hour. He had strutted from the air-raid shelter several times with purloined paint-brush and a bucket of the caretaker's gloss-paint in hand, intent upon painting the trunks of all the school trees red.

He suddenly spun about, sneering and screamed,

'I won't! And you can't make me!'

'Philip, you're not interested in art, so you don't have to join the class. But you do have to spend your time constructively, and I don't mean painting the trees red. So run along and fetch your notebook.'

He was like a berserk, hideous gnome as he broke into a frenzied dance, jigging up and down the lawn, foaming mouth in the centre of a twisted face, spitting at me and shrieking.

'You fucking old bitch! I won't do nothing. You piss off and leave me alone.'

I picked up a bucket of dirty, clay-filled water and slung it over the raging boy. Without pausing in his devil's dance he jigged over to my forgotten cup of tea and threw it at my head. I reached for a second bucket of water and drenched him again. Theoretically, this was the perfect way of dealing with a child who was totally out of control, for the shock of cold water usually brought tiny flickerings of sanity. The cold water treatment had no effect upon Philip. Rivulets of dirty water cascaded from greasy hair into his eyes and down over his saturated shirt as he spun away, thrashing up and down and flailing the air with tiny arms. Cellophane and plastic watched from the windows as I picked up a third bucket. Philip lowered his head, saliva drooling from his open mouth, and ran towards me. He aimed a kick at my crutch, missed, and sent the bucket of water showering over me. Marrie sped around the corner, shrieking,

'You fucking little bastard. When Miss MacMichael

tells you to do something you fucking well do it. Don't you dare hit Miss!'

She smashed a fist into the side of Philip's head, smattering the boy against a wall, then dived on top of him pummelling his crossed eyes and foaming mouth with tough fists. I pulled her off. Philip's eyes were swollen and beginning to close, blood gushed from his nose and mouth. Marrie picked up a tooth from the pavement and flung it at him.

'And don't leave your fucking fangs around this school. You've gotta belt him, Miss, that's what he needs.'

'I don't hit students, Marrie, you know that.'

'Well you otta.'

She hauled him up by his shirt collar and, as he dangled limply from her hand, blood drizzling from his battered face, she asked,

'Whatta'dcha tell him to do, Miss?'

'I asked him to do some handwriting in his notebook.'

Marrie shook him back and forth by the collar, then stalked towards the school, dragging him behind.

'You come in here with me, and if you don't do your fucking handwriting I'll punch your pissy head in. When Miss asks you to do something you fucking well don't argue and if you ever hit her again I'll cut your balls off.' Her voice trailed around the corner.

Plastic and cellophane disappeared from the window panes and I began to wash the blood and clay from the path. Philip was only twelve years of age and had a long sentence to serve with us. The purpose of the school, as stated to Department of Education officials, was to rehabilitate the inmates and equip them for return to a normal school, but in reality St. Steven's pupils left the institution only when they were promoted to a Borstal or upon reaching the age of sixteen. Not one single child had ever been transferred to a normal school. There was no time off for good behaviour.

Seamus knotted his bony, transparent fingers and surveyed the rows of cellophane students.

'Step forward, Timmy and Victor.'

The boys exchanged bewildered glances and slowly shuffled to the front, heads hanging.

'I weren't picking no rotten apples, Sir.'

'Shut up! I understand that you two were fighting by the gate yesterday. You know the rule. Get out the gloves.'

'We was just having a friendly argument, like, Sir, I don't want to fight nobody.'

'You should have thought of that yesterday. Get out the gloves and go out to the back.'

One of the school rules dictated that, if two boys were brawling they must don boxing gloves and fight it out. Like all the rules at St. Steven's, this one applied to some students and not to others, was spasmodically enforced according to Seamus' mood, and was in a state of constant alteration, death and rebirth. It was impossible to be aware of most rules, for they were arbitrarily created, by the Head, and hastily slain as dictated by caprice. Invisible rules were the cogs that kept St. Steven's kaleidoscopic foundations rotating in a wide, erratic journey to nowhere. Unsteady students, knotted with fear and tension, clung to the paper school, foundering in a quagmire of rotting instability, unable to know if they were obeying or breaking unimagined rules. Because the scratched Mercedes had thrown Seamus into a particularly nasty mood, one of the most vicious regulations had been unearthed, and Timmy now reluctantly trotted off for the gloves.

Boxing matches were fought on the back lawn, students forced to observe the proceeedings from the surrounding pavement. Staff watched from seats on the steps, and Seamus was enthroned on a folding chair on the topmost stair. Sickened and disgusted I refused to attend the matches, denounced for my conviction that organized fighting was only a socially approved extension of our students' tendency to resolve any problem with violence. Cloaked in the respectable word 'sport', it hindered the formation of relationships, prevented any grasp of the basic concepts of love and friendship, and reinforced the solitary, aggressive behaviour that typified our disturbed students.

'Right. Now everybody out to the lawn.'

They poured out into the milky sunlight and stationed themselves around the grass ring. Seamus ascended the steps, carefully dusted the wooden chair with his handkerchief, and sat down, crossing his sinewy, silk-encased legs. Alabaster eyes glistened as the boys began to put on the boxing gloves, and a vindictive smile twitched the corners of his thin mouth. He cracked gaunt knuckles in salacious anticipation of the forthcoming contest. I turned inside and stumbled to Una's room.

The curtains had been drawn against sight of the competition, and she sat sewing in darkened silence. Dusky corners were jammed with boys hoping to thus avoid participation in the fray. When he was in a particularly sadistic temper, Seamus refused to confine the match to the original offenders, and ordered all boys in the school to pair up and spar in turn. Those with no inclination for the sport retreated to Una's room or my air-raid shelter, knowing that we would defend and protect them.

'How long do you think it will go on today?'

Una's face contorted. 'The way he's feeling it may last all week. He won't be satisfied until everyone has a go with those bloody gloves, including the staff.'

The sound of hoarse cheers and muffled thuds drifted through the curtains. I sat in gnarled frustration and watched Una jab viciously at a piece of printed material.

'Come on, Timmy.'

'Victor, use your right! The right, you fucker!'

'You sod! Keep your left up! You're wide open.'

'Get him, Timmy. Oooh, that's it.'

'Victor, hit him back!'

Cowering boys pushed farther into the corners, wrapping themselves in a shroud of terrified invisibility.

'Time. End of round. That's all for you two. I want another pair to volunteer for the next match. Hurry up, who are the next contenders? Roy and Peter, come here and put on the gloves.'

One renegade nerve twitched in agitated dismay over my left eye as, skinless, my muscles and softened bones slopped over the table top. Una threw her needle to the floor and tore the flowered garment into shreds.

'That's what I said. He'll have them all out today.'

Corners of the room writhed in terror as the frightened boys squirmed and condensed into mounds of sweaty gooseflesh.

The door opened and Victor staggered in, sprawling on the floor in a ragged heap. Sobbing uncontrollably, Timmy followed.

'I didn't wanna fight 'im, Miss. He's me best friend. Him and me'r mates, like.'

Jerking myself from the chair I ran to Victor's side and pulled him to a sitting position. His head bobbled on an elastic band as he mumbled,

'It's me stitches that hurt, Miss. It's them old stitches. Oh, fuck, Miss, help me.' Tears began to squeeze from mutilated eyes and he rocked forward in agony. One front tooth had been knocked out and an old scar on his temple was reopened. Blood saturated his clothing and poured on to the floor. It had caked and dried in his hair and ears, welling in gummy brown mounds in the crevices of his neck. I cradled his ravaged head while Una ran to fetch cold water. The second match was well under way, judging from the sounds filtering through the drawn curtains.

'Come on, Peter, beat the shit out of him.'

'Right, Peter, the right.'

'Come on, you bastard, fight.'

Una returned with the water and Mrs. Greely. The latter scuttled to Victor and began mouthing professional assurances concerning the superficial quality of his wounds while she mopped the blood and smeared him with a bilious yellow unguent. Scar tissue reopened under the cream, revealing white bone and sagging muscle tissue. Thick blood gushed from the split, drizzling down into the boy's eye and dividing half of his face into ragged red and white strips. It dripped from his chin, and he rubbed red and white corpuscles into one dirty shirt sleeve. The darkened room pulsed as invisible students flattened against the walls, and plaster cracked as fear and knotted tension pushed for escape.

'Time! Next two boys in the ring. Move on out, now.'

'Now, ducks, I think we'll just dash off to the hospital for a little visit and have the doctor stitch this tiny cut for you. We'll ring Mum and tell her you'll be a little late for tea. No, don't pick at it, hold the piece of gauze over it. That's a lovely boy.'

'I didn't meanta hit him, Miss. Fuck, I wouldn't wanna hurt me mate.'

Supported by Mrs. Greely and Timmy, Victor surfaced through the simmering layers of tension and stumbled from the room. Una picked up a book and called to the packed corners of the room.

'Come on, boys, we'll go into Miss MacMichael's air-raid shelter and I'll read to you.'

An indistinct tangle of shapes began to emerge from the straining walls, as boys unplaited arms and legs and knocked benumbed brains into action. Pressing against the plaster, they edged towards the air-raid shelter, venetian blinds drawn over fogged eyeballs, ear drums puttied with grey adhesive fear. One by one they approached the door to the shelter and bolted through.

'I'm firing in there, Una. It's over one hundred degrees.'

'It's still healthier.'

The boys sat on lino-topped tables breathing in the

sodden humidity of temporary freedom from fear and insecurity. Una opened the book and I secured the door. We will all be sixteen someday.

CHAPTER TWENTY-TWO

Two days before the end of term, I thought they were wilder than usual but my mind was suffering from suspected school poisoning. Charred and shrivelled, it thumped uselessly from one side of my benumbed head to the other.

The lunch bell rang and students stormed into the Hall, jumping over windowsills, crowding through doors, shoving down the corridor, running in from the woods. Students on lunch duty fought over tin trays while the rest battled for seats. Lunch, as usual, was not ready. Desmond and Miles duelled with the battered trays while Philip beat upon the floor with one. Gaylord aimlessly fanned the torpid air with his tray, growling, 'Watch it, you fucker,' to the room in general.

When the hatch door was finally flung open they scrabbled for food, piling pots of potatoes, buckets of mince and bowls of carrots precariously atop the sturdy trays. As they raced for the tables, seated students vied with one another to see who could first trip one of the servers. Philip fell, his head coming to rest in a bowl of carrots. Marrie screamed.

'Ronnie did that. Get up and kick the bastard in the bollocks.'

Philip dragged himself up, grabbed the food splattered tray and hit Ronnie over the head. He was promptly thumped on the nose, and the two fell to the floor clawing at one another's eyes, while several students circled around, sweating in excitement and shouting:

'Punch-up! Punch-up!'

Marrie jumped up and down screaming:

'Go on, piss on him! Hit him again you bastard! I'll help you.'

She doubled up one fist and smashed each of them on the side of the head, then skipped backward laughing in delight.

I pulled Philip by the hair as Una dragged Ronnie's leg, disentangling the brawling boys. Standing between the two we pushed them towards separate tables. Mabel bellowed from the front of the Hall:

'Everyone sit down and eat. Sit down. We will remove the food and you will go without lunch if you can't calm down. Sit down, Marrie. Calm down and eat properly.'

Staff prowled about the room, hearing nothing but grinding teeth and gurgling throats as they began to wolf the boiled mince and lumpy mash. Desmond poked Gaylord under the table and Gaylord growled:

'Stop that, you fucker.'

Desmond poked him again and Gaylord stopped eating, glaring at the offender with vacant brown eyes.

'Jus' you wait. I'll get you.'

Another jab and Gaylord stood up, tableware in both hands, and flung his knife and fork at Desmond.

The latter, frightened, stumbled from the Hall while Gaylord, now berserk, grabbed all the knives on his table and threw them at the retreating figure. Exhausting the supply of tableware, he reached for plastic mugs, salt and pepper shakers and water pitchers, flinging them crazily about the Hall. Kicking wildly and striking at anyone within reach, he lifted his loaded plate of food. I screamed to an immobile plastic lady who wore an expression of terror:

'His plate! Get his plate!'

She didn't move and I reached forward. Gaylord

aimed the plate at my head, threw and missed. Plate and lunch struck my shoulder. Gelatinous mince, sodden potatoes and carrots slid down the front of my dress, plopping on to my soleless shoe. I squished my toes into the heap and stared down at my ruined dress. To boost my morale, and encourage neatness in the students, I always changed for lunch but now, looking at my only smart spring garment, I thought wistfully of the filthy jeans and sweat shirt in the air-raid shelter. What's the use.

Gaylord stiffened and covered his face with brown fingers as Seamus appeared in the doorway, wrapped in an immaculate suit of silence. Wrinkles scarlet, slitted lips drawn and pallid, he slithered to Gaylord, skirting the debris on the floor. Totally mute, he picked up a full plate and sent it crashing against the whitewashed wall. Orange, brown and grey drizzled over the cracked plaster, piling on the floor in a marble heap. He picked up another plate and sent it through the glass door of the bookcase. *Electronics for Young Boys* peeped coyly through gummy potatoes salted with splintered glass. Another plate of food smashed on the floor, yet another on the piano. Methodically he picked his way around the cellophane statues, shattering every plate, and covering the interior of the Hall with dripping, gelatinous garbage.

Pulling a silk handkerchief from his breast pocket, he daintily wiped his fingers.

'Now clean it up.'

He snaked back to his office.

'No, madam, the Department sees no reason to grant you recognition as a teacher.'

'I can't wear this home, Una. I'll have to wear my jeans and they're practically as bad, with all that clay and paint.'

'Never mind. I'll drive you home, but for God's sake please change. Looking at that dress is making me sick.'

As I started to pull on my jeans, muffled shouts were heard from the front of the school.

'Oh God, what now? I thought the children had all gone home by now. Should have done, anyway.'

'Probably Gaylord having a fit over his beads.'

'He seems to have forgotten them today.'

'Ha! You should have had him in your class for the entire day. I spend my time entertaining him so that he *will* forget. He'll be having tantrums all year over those damned beads. You ready?'

The front door flew open and a sturdy roadworker, face pale and horrified, stood there shaking.

'Come quick. Somebody help!'

He turned and ran down the front path, followed by Seamus, Una and myself. As we turned the corner we saw two more workmen pelting towards the school, pursued by Timmy, Stewart and Abel. The boys had commandeered shovels and were flailing at the heads and backs of the retreating men, while scattering oaths upon the quivering air. Catching sight of us, the trio stumbled to a halt, weapons clattering to the pavement, and stood with hands in pockets gazing at the sky. He won't help you now, boys. The workmen crept round and hid behind Una.

Frowning and buffing a gold ring on his silk suit Seamus said:

'Now explain.'

'Well it weren't us, see this . . .'

'Not *you*, you coon. I'm asking these gentlemen.'

One white-faced gentleman dug in his pocket for a tin of tobacco and papers. With trembling fingers he selected a thin paper, spread a bit of tobacco along the centre, and dropped it. He tried again, and succeeded in shaking the tobacco generously over the chrysanthemums. Seamus offered him a Turkish cigarette. He chose one, aimed for his mouth and jolted it into his nose. Seamus gently placed the crushed cigarette between the man's lips and lit it with his filigree lighter.

'Well, now, sir, these boys was using obscene language to the lady what drives your coach and . . .'

'That old bitch? She ain't no bloody lady.'

'Shut up.'

'You see, sir, first they blocked the drive so that the lady couldn't get out . . .'

'I hate that fucking old cow.'

'. . . and then they began to rip the bumpers off the front of the coach . . .'

'Pissy old bitch had it coming. Always a moan.'

'. . . and then she leaned out of the window and told them she was gonna report it all to you. They began to use foul language and . . .'

'Fucking hell, we don't know no pissed off foul language. Shit!'

'. . . and we stepped in and asked them to stop. That big boy jumped me mate from behind and the one with long hair kicked him in the kidneys. They took our shovels and I came in to get you.'

'You should keep your fucking nose out of our business, you bleeding bastard.'

'Shut up. What happened to the coach?'

'She buggered off, didn't she?'

Patty sat on the grass, watching the proceeedings with great interest.

'Patty, you saw all this. Why didn't you come in and get help for the men?'

'Why, Sir? I didn't think it was anything. It's normal round here, isn't it?'

'Gentlemen, allow me to apologize profusely, and assure you that it will never happen again. The rest of you get back to the Staff Room, and if you three don't march I'm going to boot the arses off you!'

I sank down on my tailbone, put on my blue lensed glasses and watched the drama. As it was a performance which I had witnessed, with minute variations, innumerable times, I was neither impressed nor interested. Seamus slithered in front of the boys in quivering wrath, puce wrinkles carved into the scaly epidermis. In a voice hoarse with rage he threatened to send them to Borstal, menaced all three with letters to their parents, and promised to keep them at St. Steven's until they were nineteen years old. As Head of special school he was empowered to retain them indefinitely, but it was a right never exercised with any student. They all left at sixteen. The threat of an extended sentence at St. Steven's was, however, a powerful weapon.

It was an empty, meaningless rehearsal on the tissue stage. The children were props, to be discarded if they did not support the star in his various roles as dictator, benefactor and authoritative father figure. Timmy, Stewart and Gaylord were essential to Seamus' every production, and would be detained and carefully preserved in their original condition, at least until they reached the age of sixteen.

Stewart lounged against the doorjamb, chomping insolently on a matchstick, confident that he was necessary in the drama at St. Steven's, and despising himself for his contribution. Timmy's face mirrored his guilt and dejection on the night of the moped incident, while Abel was a parody of injured innocence.

'That's all for now. You may leave, and go straight home!'

Seamus turned in dismissal and dusted his armchair with an initialled linen handkerchief. Stewart spat out the matchstick, flung an obscene sign at Seamus' bent backside and slunk towards the front door.

'Sorry, Sir.' Timmy stood for a moment and, when Seamus ignored the apology, turned and pelted down the corridor with Abel on his heels.

They sat, hands folded over well-stuffed stomachs, wearing righteous expressions. Una and I rose to leave just as the telephone rang.

Seamus replaced the telephone receiver and began to fill a platinum cigarette case. He paused and polished the embossed coat of arms on the cover, rapped it shut and tapped it on the table.

'That was the Law on the phone. They've arrested Marrie for shoplifting, along with three of the other girls here. They did eight shops before they were caught. Best shops in the borough too. Those slags have real taste. P.C. Roberts says that they've been shoplifting every day after school for months now. I'll get the others off in court, but not Marrie. That bitch has been rocking my boat here and I promise you she's away this time. She's as good as in Borstal this minute. I won't have scruff like that at my school. You all go on home now so I can get down to writing Marrie's Court Report. I'll knock that magistrate out of his fat chair.'

Seamus held one hand at arm's length and critically studied the polished nails. He frowned and blew an infinitesimal speck of dust from the index finger, then took a gold-backed buffer from one trouser pocket. With great care he added further gloss to the offensive fingernail.

'Get ready for your happy holidays in the South of France, and be prepared for some changes in classes next term. I want to try something new here. Can't get stale and stagnant.'

They beamed.

I crawled out of the front door, school bag clenched between my teeth.

'Aren't you coming in the car?'

'No thanks. I changed my mind. I'm walking.'

'Don't be daft Conor. It's miles. Come on, jump in and I'll run you home.'

'It's all right, Una. Thanks anyway.'

My liquid mind skipped through the brass ring and dripped into a circle on the pavement. It solidified and froze as cellophane statues, towed by Marrie, Victor, Stewart and Timmy skated round and round its circumference. They slid under doorways marked 'Borstal' and emerged again riding on stolen mopeds and wearing hot clothing. They slipped through a doorway marked 'School' and tumbled around the other side wearing bank messengers' uniforms. Round and round, in one door and out the other they sped on a smooth, unbroken halo of worthless brain matter.

I plaited my nerves, tied the ends with a rubber band and pressed my emotions dry. Picking up my school bag I revolved down the High Street.

Home.

THE END

THE HAND-REARED BOY BY BRIAN W. ALDISS

'It is laid out skilfully, showing a firm and confident narrative gift. It's concerned, almost exclusively, with Horace Stubbs's sexuality, which is obsessive – and why not? Horry, after all, is at the age when sexuality IS obsessive – and with his plunging efforts to satisfy imperious lusts. Yet it isn't really pornographic; Aldiss's purposes are manifestly sincere, sometimes serious, sometimes lustily comic.' – *The Times*

0 552 08651 7 65p

EVEN COWGIRLS GET THE BLUES BY TOM ROBBINS

The novel of the year with the cast of the century!

Starring *Sissy Hankshaw* – flawlessly beautiful, almost. A small-town girl with big-time dreams and thumbs to match – hitchhiking her way into your heart, your hopes and your sleeping bag . . .

Featuring: *Bonanza Jellybean* and the smooth-riding cowgirls of Rubber Rose Ranch. *Chink*, lascivious guru of yams and yang. *The Countess*, homosexual tycoon of feminine hygiene; *Julian*, Mohawk by birth; asthmatic aesthete and husband by disposition.

Dr Robbins, preventive psychiatrist and reality instructor . . .

Follow Sissy's amazing hitchhiking odyssey as she sets forth on a series of intellectual and erotic adventures that will bring tears to your eyes.

0 552 10513 9 95p